# The Crow House

## JEAN ATKIN

Published in 2013 by FeedARead.com Publishing – Arts Council funded

A CIP catalogue record for this title is available from the British Library.

Front cover drawing © Alex Stone

Other illustrations from 'Galloway Gossip Sixty Years Ago'

By Dr R Trotter (1877)

*The Crow House* first published 2012 by Biscuit Tin Press

About the author

Jean Atkin wrote 'The Crow House' because Wigtown's wide street, Georgian bookshops and blue estuary got inside her head and wouldn't go away. This is a place where all the stones have stories.

Jean Atkin lived in Dumfries and Galloway for twelve years but is now settled in Shropshire. She is a published and award-winning poet and works as a writer in education.

www.thecrowhouse.wordpress.com

# 1   Scotland's Book Town

Holly was bored by the journey, but not keen to arrive. She watched the smooth passage of rust and purple hills that shimmered above the estuary.  The car swept below them, obedient to the bends and the rise and fall of the narrow road.  She could feel her dad's  concentration on the hot road, and on the house they were going to.

She knew he was uneasy.  Stan's big hands were capable on the steering wheel, but she could feel his worries with them in the car just as if they were passengers in the back seat. He wasn't doing much talking.

Back in Carlisle, Holly had liked Liddy. She was funny, and friendly, but not pushy.  She had made Stan laugh, and Holly had thought that anyone who could do that again must be at least reasonably good news.

Now, as the miles passed, Holly felt reality sink in.  She was to stay with Liddy and Callum, and there'd be no Stan till the end of August.  She would get dropped off today, and then Stan would drive back to Carlisle for the rest of the summer.  When he had sold the Carlisle business he could move in too.   Then they would be a family of four in Wigtown, Galloway.

She and Stan would leave the house in Carlisle. Forever.  Her mum's house.

Holly switched her thoughts quickly away.

Liddy was ok.

It was important to keep that in mind. Stan had been sad long enough.

Holly wondered about Callum. Callum had met Stan, and then refused to meet Holly. Nobody had said so, but that was obviously what had happened. Callum was twelve. At least she would be the eldest.

And at least she wasn't abandoned. If her mum had left her, it was because she had died, not because, like Callum's dad, he'd just gone off.

Or so Holly supposed. Stan had just said, "No, Callum doesn't see his dad." End of story. Though of course it wasn't.

The sea was silver. It speared back through the green land on her left.

"You ok Holly?" Stan glanced quickly at her, and back at the road.

"Yes. I'm going to live in a bookshop, remember." She felt heroic.

"That's my girl." Stan drove up a hill and past a big signpost.

"Wigtown - Scotland's Book Town," he read off the signpost. "What a beautiful place. What a sight. Just look at those mountains the other side of Wigtown Bay." He waved a hand leftwards across the bay to the hills.

Holly didn't say anything.

The car slowed down to make the corner onto North Main Street, where Callum and Liddy lived, and Holly

6

stopped thinking about the big stuff, to concentrate on the tricky present.

Wigtown's wide street of bookshops was quiet in the warm sun of a Wednesday afternoon. Stan parked outside the bookshop that belonged to Liddy.

Holly opened the passenger door and climbed stiffly out of the car. She stretched, and looked up into the blue sky. She caught a glimpse of a face at an upstairs window.

As she looked, the face vanished, drawn back into the room.

Callum.

The wide, white-painted front door stood open between its Georgian pillars. There was a brass plaque to one side which said, in handsome Roman capitals

## GOOD GARDEN BOOKS
### No. 71

Liddy emerged, her red plait swinging over her shoulders, a scarf fluttering.

"Stan, Holly, how lovely to see you! How was the journey? Have you eaten?"

She gave Holly a quick squeeze around the shoulders and a friendly sidelong smile before moving close to Stan. Their kiss was not too long, but intimate. Holly looked away. She reminded herself she didn't mind. Liddy was probably just what her sad dad needed.

Callum was another matter.

7

He was standing just inside the door. He was watching his mother and Stan with revulsion.

"Hi" said Holly, to test him.

Callum said nothing.

They all went in through a light, wide, cool hall. It had ornate plasterwork around the ceiling. Holly passed a room to her left and glimpsed through an open door a tall marble fireplace and shelf after shelf of books. Liddy led the way past the foot of a curving staircase into a café in the back room where a few customers were seated at little tables, under more bookshelves. They browsed in their books, mugs of coffee by their elbows. Liddy grinned quickly at Stan and Holly, raising her eyebrows.

Then she swept them all across the café towards another door on which there was a wonkily hand painted sign that said, "Private".

Liddy opened it. They followed her through a big untidy kitchen and into the dappled shade of a conservatory, where she settled everyone around a table.

Holly stared around her with cautious approval. The conservatory was an old one. Dark green paint flaked off its metal frame. Peering up through a canopy of vine leaves she could see a line of metal spears along the ridge of the conservatory, and blue sky. The door stood propped open, giving a glimpse of a long, walled back garden. There was a green cloth on the table.

"There's warm bread, cheese and salad", Liddy said.

"Let me give you a hand." Stan edged round the table and followed Liddy back into the kitchen.

8

Holly looked across at Callum.

Callum glared at her.

Holly shrugged and looked away. She sat down.

"Are you pleased to get out of school early then Holly?" Liddy came back into the conservatory and settled herself. She passed Holly the butter, and began to serve herself some salad.

Holly took it and smiled at Liddy, avoiding Callum's gaze.

"Certainly am". She pretended to consider. "I don't really think I'll miss it much. Though I'll miss my friends. Hopefully they can come and visit."

"Of course they can." Liddy's voice was warm. "It's really not that far to Carlisle."

"What's the school like here?" Holly asked. "Where is it anyway?"

"Newton Stewart," Liddy said, "By bus. And Callum's just finished S1, so he's the one with the cutting edge information."

"Yes, what's the verdict Callum?" Stan joined in, grinning at Callum in a friendly manner.

Callum folded his arms, leaned back in his chair, looked straight at Stan and remained mutinously silent.

"Callum". Liddy put out a hand towards his arm. "Callum."

He shrugged her off, shoved his chair back with a screech and went out of the conservatory into the garden. Holly saw him thrust his hands into his pockets. His shoulders hunched as he walked away.

9

"I'm sorry Stan. And Holly." Liddy looked upset. "He's not really come round to things yet."

"Oh, don't worry. It's understandable". Stan reached out a long arm and hugged Liddy. "He'll get used to it. Holly's an easy-going type. She'll be the soul of tact for a few weeks, won't you Holly love?" He let go of Liddy and gave his daughter's hair an affectionate tug.

Holly shook herself free and sighed. They both looked at her hopefully. Holly smiled wearily at them because they were depending on her. She picked up her bread, and took a bite. Callum was clearly going to be a major pain, and all the effort was obviously going to have to come from her. And the adults were sitting there hoping she knew something about enraged, jealous twelve year old boys that they didn't.

Liddy began her salad, but eyed Holly anxiously.

"He'll come back in when he's ready. I did have one good idea Holly. You can ride a pony, can't you?"

Mouth full, Holly hesitated, then nodded.

"There is a pony," Liddy went on, "Well he's mine. He's not in his first youth. He could do with some exercise, and I don't have time at the moment. He might cheer up your summer."

"Brilliant!" exclaimed Stan, "Holly loves riding, never been able to do enough of it have you love?"

"Thanks" said Holly politely. "That'd be fun".

But she cheered up fractionally. Liddy got up and left the room, returning with a small framed photo in her hand.

"This is him. He's called Drum". She passed the photo to Holly.

10

Holly saw a yellow-coloured pony looking at the camera from under a long dark forelock. He was sturdy, and shaggy looking. There was a jauntiness about him that appealed to her. She peered closer.

"I had an idea Stan", Liddy was saying. There was laughter in her voice. "A new name for the business. With you coming in, I thought we could re-launch it as "Berry Good Garden Books"".

Holly winced. Stan Berry roared with laughter, hugged Liddy again and started talking about the secondhand bookshop trade and what he would be able to do to help Liddy get more online business once he'd sold up his shop in Carlisle. Holly Berry stared at the picture of Drum, not seeing him any more. That was all she needed, moving to a new place and a new school. Her name was a bit of a sore point. She mostly forgot it, but other people found it all too entertaining, at least on first acquaintance. Stan admitted he had been responsible for it, thirteen years ago. "At least we didn't call you Rasp!" he would grin.

If Liddy shared this sense of humour, then things were a bit worse than Holly had thought.


"I'll be in my room," Callum said without looking at anyone as he stumped past Liddy and Holly in the hall. Following after Liddy, Holly let her hand glide up the broad curve of the dark wood banister, enjoying its smooth coolness. It was topped with an acorn where it met the landing.

Before her, in front of a tall landing window with a border of blue stained glass, stood an oval table. An old silk scarf was draped across it as a tablecloth, and on the scarf was a curious collection of objects: some green glass fishing floats, a bunch of antique keys on a big iron ring, and a sheep's skull, made huge by three curls of ram's horns. Holly stared at them, vaguely curious. Then she hurried after Liddy.

"Here you are then Holly." Liddy was waiting beside a door. As Holly arrived she pushed it open.

"Make yourself at home in here, while I try and find a civilised being under the stroppy exterior of my son".

"Good luck" muttered Holly aloud, as Liddy whisked back round the door. Holly heard her footsteps receding down the long landing. She sat down on the edge of the bed, and looked around her.

The room, she had to admit, was quite nice actually.

It was large, and square, and it seemed to have the same flea market approach to decoration as the oval table. A dressmaker's dummy stood against one wall, topped with a broad brimmed hat from some distant decade. It had strings of beads hung round its neck. Worn green velvet curtains festooned a large and very ancient looking window which overlooked North Main Street.

Holly went to it, and looked down at the neatness of the bowling green and the railings around the quiet gardens in the centre of Wigtown. The other side of the street was quite weirdly far away. She supposed there must once have been a broad market place or something in the middle. Downhill to her left was an extraordinary building, much bigger than everything else. It was like a stocky French chateau in red stone, with a handsome clock tower. Craning her neck she could just see the big hills on the far side of Wigtown Bay.

She stared down at the roof of Stan's car, parked below. He had to go straight back to Carlisle. Business. Mind you, the way Callum was behaving, he was probably grateful to.

A sense of awful loneliness overwhelmed Holly. "My life is changing. It's changing right now," she thought. "I can't stop it. My flipping dad".

A tear leaked out and rolled down her cheek.

Holly turned and stared sadly into a mirror over an old fashioned dressing table, watching herself being unhappy like she might watch a stranger at a railway station. She saw a rounded face, fair-skinned and freckled, the skin reddening rapidly around light-coloured grey eyes. She did not think she was pretty even when she wasn't crying. Her dark, heavy hair fell forward over her cheeks, looking pale green in the shadowy bedroom. She could be underwater.

There was a knock at the door.

A boy's voice announced gruffly, "Ma says your dad's got to go after they've had a cup of tea. Do you want one."

It wasn't a question.

He didn't want an answer.

Holly, embarrassed at the mere possibility of being found crying by Callum, sprang away from the mirror, wiping her eyes hastily.

"I'm coming", she said, trying to sound completely normal and not very friendly.

13

When she got down to the conservatory again, Callum was there. He gave her a quick look, then stared down at the tablecloth.

Stan was tipping up the last of his mug of tea. He put it down, and rose to his feet.

"I'll text you every day," he said to Holly. "Hey, don't look like that – you'll set me off too -" Holly scowled horribly – "Can't be helped, I can't wait to get through this summer and move in with you all properly – but it won't half help if I get the business sold and arrive with some money. I should be able to get down some weekends."

Then he was hugging Holly, then Liddy, and even reached out a hand towards Callum before tactfully dodging and scooping up his car keys instead.

They stood on the warm steps and waved him off.


"I'm so pleased we finally found it for you, yes...see you again soon, goodbye...goodbye."

Liddy gently ushered out the last customer and closed the heavy street door to the shop. With a sigh she shot the bolts, top and bottom, and straightened up.


"There. If anyone wants out during the evening, we use the back door and the path to the pend down the side of the neighbour's. Callum'll show you."

Holly noticed Liddy did not look at Callum as she said this. Holly stole a quick glance at him as Liddy came back

14

into the hall, carefully closing the inner half glass door behind her.

Callum's face just looked closed, bleak. His mother consulted her watch, then took Callum firmly but gently by the shoulders.

"I'm off to make your favourite dinner Callum. While I do that, can you show Holly the shop, and the garden and the pend, so she starts to know her way around. It's a beautiful evening."

"Okay." Callum shrugged himself free, and then impulsively turned back and hugged his mother. Holly saw Liddy stop, and wrap her arms briefly round him. Her eyes met Holly's for a moment over Callum's back.

Then she released him, and disappeared in the direction of the kitchen. Callum looked after her for a second, then turned his gaze on Holly.

His eyes were dark brown and wary. Holly waited. He stuck his hands into his pockets.

"This," he intoned heavily, like a depressed tour guide, "is the bookshop. It's a place where people come who want to buy books. On your right," he waved his arm at the door on the right hand side of the hall, "is the room with books about the technicalities of gardening. Known as the How To Room. When you feel the need to find out about pruning, grafting and weeding, that's where you go. It's surprising how many people do."

He paused.

Then he turned and opened the door on the other side of the hall, and Holly followed him into the room with the

15

tall fireplace. "Here you find the room with the books about the history of gardening, which is known as the Gardening History Room. Who created the great gardens of the past. What they used to do with the poisonous herbs they cultivated. Who they did it to."

Holly looked at him. He was deadpan.

She deferred judgement, and to distract him, asked, "What's in the glass case? Is it valuable?"

"Why do you think it's locked up?" He did not meet her eyes, but mooched grumpily towards a table bearing a glass case of the kind still found in traditional museum displays.

"Hey, it's a book!" Holly exclaimed, peering into the glass case.

She saw Callum's eyebrows rise.

"Hey, it's a bookshop!" he said nastily.

She ignored him.

"How old is it? 'The Grete - is that right – like 'Great' - ? – The Grete Herball'" she read from the embossed title on the book's grand leather binding.

"Printed in 1809. By one Doctor Jared Sliddery." Callum informed her. "And under Liddy's law, no-one's allowed to open this case unless she's there".

Holly stared at the book blankly. Something nudged uneasily at her mind.

"Is it a valuable book then?" she asked.

"It's kind of interesting. Old Sliddery used to live here," said Callum.

"And Liddy found the book in the house?" said Holly.

Callum looked taken aback.

"Well, yes, as a matter of fact she did". He stared at her more closely. "How did you know?"

Holly had no idea, but the room felt too hot, and she put up a hand and rubbed one of her eyes suddenly, turning away to avoid Callum's curiosity and her own discomfort.

"Where does that littler door lead to?" She gestured back out into the hall.

Callum led the way out of the Gardening History room and went to it and rattled the latch. "Ma keeps it locked. It goes down to the basement, where it's cold and shadowy and spooky."

She saw him check to see what effect he was having on her, so she took care to show no reaction.

"She stores stuff down there."

"Don't the books get damp then?" Holly asked.

"Who said it was books? Who said it was damp?" Callum walked away from her through the café and opened the door that said "Private". Holly sighed and followed him. They passed Liddy stirring something on the stove, and she smiled at them anxiously.

"And this is the garden." Callum stood by the conservatory door and waved his hand grandly. He was obviously furious.

"Callum" Holly tried, "I didn't have much say about – stuff - either, you know."

"And this," he said, striding away up the path, "you may be able to identify as a back gate. Which leads" he opened it and walked through "to a back lane, known to those of us who actually belong in Wigtown, as a pend".

Holly followed him, fed up.

He showed her the turning where the pend became a narrow passage leading out under a gated arch between two tall houses to meet North Main Street.

He demonstrated exactly how to operate the bolt which secured the gate.

Then he said nothing at all as they turned back to No. 71 to sit down to Callum's favourite dinner.


It turned out to be homemade Shepherd's Pie with new carrots and peas Liddy said she had picked from the garden that afternoon.

The food was good. Callum appeared to be sulking. Liddy chatted to Holly about the pony, Drum.

"I had him from when I was a teenager," she explained. "I always expected I'd have to sell him, but somehow I've managed not to."

"So I suppose he must be quite old by now?" asked Holly, realising just too late that this might not be the best thing to say. She looked down at her plate, and speared a few peas.

But Liddy just grinned. "Well, he's no longer young! He must be getting on for twenty two. But he's fit and healthy, quite rideable. I wouldn't jump him any more, or trot long distances on a hard road, but for hacking about on, especially with you up, he won't feel it."

Holly imagined herself riding along beside Wigtown Bay on just such a golden summer evening. She smiled at Liddy.

"Where do you keep him?  Can I fetch him myself?"

"I've asked Alison to mind the shop tomorrow morning."  Liddy was smiling too.  "I thought I'd take you down to his field to help you catch him and get you started. In the summer, Callum's used to fending for himself and finding things to do, because I can't take much time away from the bookshop. Alison helps me out."  She put down her fork and looked anxiously at Holly.  "I hope that's alright Holly.  Your dad said you were very good at looking after yourself.  But perhaps you'd rather you didn't have to."

Holly shot Liddy a surprised look.  As if she hadn't noticed, Liddy continued, "Drum's good to catch.  Mostly. He'd like to go out, he gets a bit bored these days."

After the meal, they took a short walk, at Liddy's suggestion ("And you can come too, Callum"), out through the pend and down North Main Street towards the pink chateau, which Liddy said was the County Buildings.  An unbelievably boring name, Holly thought.

They walked past the edge of the graveyard, and looked out over the bay.

"It's not really a bay at all," she said, puzzled.

She saw the estuary gleam like a curving snake through bright green marshes where sheep grazed.

"That's low water," said Liddy, "It fills up when the tide comes in.  How much it fills up depends on the time of year too.  That's Cairnsmore of Fleet on the other side."

Liddy was pointing to the largest of the hills that ranged all the way along the horizon above the bay. Cairnsmore bulked impassive in the stretching chain of hills,

19

its summit a mass of stone, the lower slopes purpled with heather.

Some other people were out walking in Wigtown too, because it was a beautiful evening. But to Holly, used to living in a city, it was almost disturbingly quiet.

Trudging upstairs later, past the table with the glass fishing floats and the ram's skull, she felt tired out.

She lay in bed staring at the unfamiliar grapes and vine leaves of the plaster cornicing that ran round the room below the ceiling, then fell heavily asleep.

# 2    The 9th Day of March, in the Year of our Lord, 1797, in The Crow House, Wigtowne.

*She watches him write, even though the letters are only shapes to her. It is another magic, how he can make the marks on parchment with his thick dark quill. He is binding his thoughts to the surface, so they are always there, for ever and ever. She is very afraid of him, but she knows her place. And her place is to stand by the door, to wait without fidgeting until she is needed.*

*"The horehound" he says, without looking up.*

*She has been trained, and fetches him the bowl of ground dried leaves from the other table. She is a little proud that she can identify the herbs so easily by their smell, and by their texture. She places the bowl silently on his table, by his right hand. She steps back.*

*His long, white finger stirs the leaves.*

*"Vinegar." His voice is always cold.*

*She obeys, but the jug is heavy and as she lowers it to the table a single drop splashes from the lip.*

*"Idiot girl!"*

*He lashes out at her, anger flaring in his narrow eyes. "You are unteachable. Lucky for you the day that I took you*

21

*in, but what a toll you have exacted from me with your carelessness and your foolishness."*

*She hangs her head. She takes care to stay just out of reach. She keeps her eyes down, always down, but she can feel his glare raking her contemptuously.*

*"No decent people in this town would have you," he reminds her. His voice grates on her ears. "As you bear the Mark, so is your nature fixed." He sighed. " Yet in Christian charity I took you in, and so must bear this cross with patience. Stand by the door." He bends again over his work.*

*Time passes. She stands by the door. She is biting her lip, gnawing at it, her hands tight clasped behind her back, fingers interlaced. What he says is true. She bears the Mark. She is evil.*

# 3  Way Too Optimistic

The sun hadn't come into her room yet, but the brightness of the day glowed promisingly around the edge of the heavy green curtains. Holly pushed hair out of her eyes, and sat up slowly.

Her brain felt slow, fogged with books. The smell of them, musty, leather-bound, ancient, was filling her head.

She shook it, rubbed her eyes, and got out of bed. The big house was quiet. She opened her door.

Nothing, but the enticing smell of bacon. The book dream receded.

Mindful of the promised ride on Drum, Holly put on her jeans and a t-shirt and made her way down the wide stairs. Through the old, uneven glass of the landing window, Wigtown's roofs lay dreaming in the morning sun. Holly made her way into the kitchen, the wonky "Private" sign flapping on the door as she closed it behind her.

"Morning, Holly. You're up early. Is that as usual or the result of being in a new place?" Liddy wondered, flipping bacon over in the frying pan on the top of the Rayburn.

"I've always done it." Holly seated herself at the table. She searched for something to say.

"What about you?"

"Oh, I can get up early" Liddy looked quickly sideways at Holly, while sliding fried egg and bacon onto a plate. "Not

23

usually Callum though. And you came down at exactly the right moment." She passed the plate.

"Thanks." Holly took it and put it down in front of her.

"Does Callum take after his dad then?"

She suddenly realised this might be a bit personal. She picked up her knife and fork and concentrated on puncturing the egg. A stream of rich yellow yolk flowed slowly across the white, then bumped down the step made by the toast, and onto the plate. She scooped it back.

"Maybe," said Liddy obscurely. She took a plate of bacon and eggs for herself and sat down. She gave a quick sigh, then cut into her toast, arranged a piece of egg on it, and ate it. She continued.

"Callum can't get up early without significant effort. But he can do long division and unbug the computer, which is certainly more than I can. Do you think you're like your mum?"

Holly chewed and considered. "My dad says I look like her. I can't see it though."

Holly did not say she thought her mother had been pretty, in case Liddy thought she was fishing for compliments. She carried on.

"I was eight when she - she was just – my mum."

She saw Liddy was looking at her very gently and to distract from the moment she added, "Dad says she could read Latin, haggle in markets, brew beer and tell the future." It was what she usually said when the subject of her mum came up with people she didn't know very well. She stopped,

24

worried now that she had just made her mum seem like a hard act to follow. She cut up bacon.

Liddy seemed unfazed though. "And which of those can you do?" She did her nice sidelong smile thing at Holly again. Holly was smiling back, when she remembered that Stan probably liked that smile too.

"I can tell the future" Callum stepped suddenly and very quietly around the kitchen door. "In the next minute, I will get a plate of bacon and eggs. My mother will be cheerful to me, and Holly will be tactful. I will eat my breakfast then get out of here and go to Will's for the day. And you see I can get out of bed when I want to."

Holly stared at him and Callum said, "I got that wrong. Holly will be gobsmacked, and then tactful."

Liddy scowled at him. "Don't push your luck Callum. I could put you on dusting duty."

"Dusting duty...?" Holly couldn't keep up.

"The unglamorous side of keeping a shop" Liddy explained. "Not all customers are happy with the real grime of the second-hand book." She piled up Holly's plate on her own, placed a full one in front of Callum and lowered the lid on the Rayburn. "Looks like you've finished Holly. Let's go and find Drum. I've got time to be with you this morning. Callum, you'll be back by 4.30, ok?"

Callum, mouth full, nodded. Liddy led Holly out of the kitchen, pausing in the scullery to lift down a riding hat, a saddle and a bridle.

They walked together down the garden path, past vegetable beds and clumps of rather unruly herbs. At the gate Liddy passed the bridle over to Holly and undid the bolt.

"Here, you can carry this. He goes fine on a snaffle these days, but he was quite onward bound once."

Holly was relieved to see the bridle did look quite a simple one, without any extra chains and straps, which she vaguely associated with the kind of pony she would rather not get on.

The main street was warm and dusty and Holly could see the newsagents just opening. A man came out and propped up a billboard with a newspaper headline on it. Liddy waved to him across the broad street, and he waved back. They walked on downhill past the County Buildings and the graveyard.

"It looks very old," Holly remarked politely, nodding over scrambling ivy at the still presence of weathered headstones.

"It is." Liddy hitched up the saddle in her arms. "Ask Callum to show you, there are strange old gravestones in there from the time of the Covenanters." She glanced at Holly and measured understanding.

"The Covenanters were persecuted for their faith, um, in the seventeenth century. They fell out with the rest of the Church, and groups of them used to worship on the hill tops. The government decided they were trouble and used soldiers to hunt them down, and quite a few of them ended up martyred. Right here in Wigtown, two women, an old one and a young one, were imprisoned in the Martyrs' Cell under the County Buildings, then tied to a stake and left to drown in Wigtown Bay".

"Urgh!" said Holly.

"Well probably they were a bit fanatical too, in their way" grinned Liddy. She quickened her pace. "As it happens, Drum lives in a little field down near the Martyrs' Stake".

The pony had heard them. Holly saw his head thrust over the top of the gate as they walked down the lane, and he whinnied.

"Hello beautiful, are you bored?" Liddy put the saddle on the gate and opened it, gesturing to Holly to follow her. The pony turned briskly to meet them, his muzzle stretched out greedily.

"He gets one. One pony nut. Or he starts nipping people." Liddy gave it to him and put an arm over his neck. "Pass the reins over his head Holly. That's it, got you now mate".

Drum stood placidly, licking his lips over his single pony nut, while Liddy supervised Holly putting on the bridle.

"Just don't let go!" Liddy showed Holly an rusting tin trunk sitting cockeyed in the hedgerow. It contained a headcollar and rope, a brush and a hoofpick. They slipped the headcollar loosely over Drum's bridle, and tied him to the gate.

"He's a good pony, but a pony" Liddy said, as they took it in turns to brush dried mud from Drum. "I mean, he would take advantage. But he's fairly well mannered if you remind him firmly."

27

"What colour do you call him?" Holly asked, crouching to brush vigorously at stubbornly ingrained mud on one of Drum's hocks.

"He's dun. A yellow dun with grey in his coat, so he can at best -" Liddy smiled down at Holly, "- look rather attractively silvery. He has a dorsal stripe down his back to his tail, and black legs with some striping like a zebra near his knees. He must be part Highland, probably, to be this colour."

Holly stood, and admired the pony. He was a little long in the back, though sturdy, with black feather on his legs and strong black feet. His mane and forelock were abundant, and his tail, although thick and set high, was a little short, falling to only just below his hocks. His eye glinted darkly at her through his thick, black, sweet-scented forelock. His head was rather large. He put out his nose, and then nudged her strongly.

"Manners, Drum!" said Liddy, shoving him back.

They saddled him and led him out of the field, where Holly managed to mount without embarrassing herself.

Liddy directed Holly along a lane below the town, with long views across Wigtown Bay to the hills. Holly demonstrated successfully that she could rise to the trot, and heave Drum's head up when he tried to graze in the wavy sweetness of the grass verges. After about half an hour Liddy said, "You're going to be fine with him," in such approving tones that Holly warmed with pleasure.

They turned off onto a green lane that led back towards the Martyrs' Stake, which, when they'd arrived there, turned out to be not a stake but an inscribed stone telling the story of the two women's fate.

"Would the tide really have reached them here?" wondered Holly. Sheep grazed the salt marshes all around, and the estuary seemed far out in the bay.

"It would have then," said Liddy.

They put Drum back into his field, and Liddy kept Holly laughing with stories of his past misdeeds all the way back up into Wigtown, pausing only to take her briefly inside the County Buildings to see the small, whitewashed Martyrs Cell, with its small, barred window and thick metal door.


Later, Callum pushed his bike into the shed next to Liddy's then stood irresolute in the garden. Will's sympathy for his situation had been brief. Will was the happy product of two happy parents. His point of view was way too optimistic for Callum.

He set off indoors, intending to communicate as little as possible till bedtime.

# 4    Foule Humores

Trudging downstairs the next morning at just after ten, Callum caught the sound of Liddy's laughter from the kitchen, followed by giggling from Holly. He stopped on the stairs, and scowled. The disturbance to his home fanned out from the cheerful voices, like radio waves passing through walls and ceilings, up through the soles of his feet.

Slowly he continued down the last steps. He decided to ignore, for the time being, his need for breakfast, and skulk in the Gardening History Room. He reckoned that with luck Holly would collect the tack and go out to catch Drum as soon as she'd eaten her breakfast. Which would leave the coast clear.

He pushed the tall door quietly closed behind him. The room smelled comfortingly of old paper and leather bindings. Callum wandered around the bookcases, and peered stealthily out of the window, hoping to see Holly emerge from the pend, burdened with saddlery.

No such luck.

Drifting past the table with the glass case, he was struck by both curiosity and rebellion. He fished in the drawer for the key, and unlocked the top of the case.

This was strictly forbidden by Liddy.

Callum lifted the glass lid, and settled it carefully back as far as its hinges would allow.

The Grete Herball lay grandly in the safety of the case, not a very large book, but thick and impressively bound in high quality tooled leather, with gilt decoration. He bent his head and sniffed appreciatively. Then he did the banned thing, and opened the covers.

His fingers touched thick creamy paper with soft hand-cut edges, but the first few were blank.

Cautiously aware of the delicacy of the old paper between his finger and thumb, Callum turned another page. He read:

**THE GRETE HERBALL**

**OF**

**JARED SLIDDERY, HERMETIC DOCTOR**

**OF WIGTOWNE,**

**IN THE COUNTY OF GALLOWAY**

Heavy woodcuts showed the sinuous growth of plants up either side of the title page. Callum lifted the book a little under its spine to ease the binding, and the heavy pages riffled past his face to fall open at a page further on. He read:

"Where chamber is sweeped, and wormwood is strowne no flea for his life dar abide to be known."

Right.

Further down he caught the word "Amulets", and bent to read the print:

"Be on your guard gentil reader, for those Conjurors, bad Physitians, lewd Chirugians, Melancholick Witches and Coseners who would recommend you falfe Pomanders and Amulets againft Foule humores".

He remembered Liddy telling him that an unexpected 'f' in the middle of a word in old books meant an 's'.

Beside this warning was a woodcut showing a kindly faced man standing over a workbench on which were piled bowls of seeds and leaves, small pans, a tabletop brazier, a chopping board and knives.

Callum looked into the man's eyes. They were no longer kind.

The picture in the book seemed to tilt out into the room, and the scent of lavender, mingled with something harsher and earthier, flowed into his nostrils. He swayed, feeling suddenly sick and faint.

His head cleared again.

He saw that he was standing on a polished oak plank floor, which seemed to have replaced Liddy's worn Persian rug.

The man at the table stopped chopping up herbs, and looked up.

But he looked right through Callum, his eyes shifting around the room to the closed door, and then he bent over his work again. His face was deeply lined between nose and mouth in a way that made him look hungry.

"He can't see me", thought Callum.

The man's long, pale fingers slowly scattered dark leaves into a steaming pot. He sniffed the aroma as it rose, and nodded slowly.

Callum felt his heart crashing unevenly inside his chest. He edged sideways towards the door, watching the man all the time. As he grasped the doorknob and twisted it, the hinges creaked.

At once the man straightened towards the sound, his lips thinning.

"He can't see me – *but he can hear me!*" Callum, panicking now, caught the door open and lunged out through it.

He heard the man step away from the table to follow him, and flung himself forward, colliding violently with Liddy in the hall.

"Oough! Callum! Slow down!"

He looked over her freckled arm, and back through the part-open door where tranquil sunshine slanted across the Gardening History Room in his mother's bookshop.

# 5    Spitting on the Knife

*The shutters being once closed against the darkening evening, she turns to the fireplace.  She sets down her bucket, brush and hand shovel, and crouches by the hearth. The room is still generously lit by two handsome wall sconces bearing three candles each, but she is in her own shadow as she kneels in front of the fire.*

*She sets aside a half burned log to use again and shovels out ashes into the bucket.  Carefully, she re-lays the fire to be lit first thing in the morning.*

*She steps carefully around Doctor Sliddery's fine rug with the bucket of ashes, and lowers it down by the door, before returning to the workbench to clean the tools of his trade.*

*Taking a rag tucked into her pinafore (whose condition is scarcely distinguishable from it), she cleans out the many small bowls that litter the table.  She winnows flakes of dried leaves onto its polished wood, and when she has finished she gathers them carefully up in her hand, and puts them into the fireplace on top of the ready-laid fire.*

*She returns to the workbench, but more reluctantly now.  And stands, her gaze fixed on his knife.  It is lying near the back.  The inlaid silver on its handle catches the light.*

*On its blade are stains, blue-black and crusted red-brown.*

*It must be cleaned.*

*Slowly she extends a hand towards it. For luck, her other hand grips her Red. She keeps it hidden in her pocket for occasions like this.*

*As she picks up the knife, she is holding her breath.*

*Now she has it.*

*She spits. Once on the blade and once to protect herself. Then, careful of the blade's edge, she cleans the knife on the rag.*

*She replaces it on the bench and sighs audibly.*

*She picks up the full ash bucket and is gone, closing the tall door softly after her. The door knob turns, and clicks into place.*

# 6    Clary, for Clear-Eye

The late July sunshine warmed Holly's back as she jogged along the track above the salt marshes. Drum's small curved ears were pricked forward, he was enjoying himself. Holly rose to the trot, a little too bouncy in the saddle, but triumphant.

After a fortnight of being helped, today she had not needed Liddy or Callum at all. Drum had come obligingly when she shouted for him, allowed himself to be caught and saddled, and they were now successfully skirting the edge of Wigtown together.

The pony slowed his pace and dropped into a walk. Holly patted him enthusiastically on the neck, and Drum gave a heavy sigh, stretching down his yellow and silver neck and half-heartedly shaking his mane. He took the opportunity to step sideways and snatch a mouthful of grass as he did so, and Holly heaved belatedly on the reins to stop him.

She drove him on with her legs, kicking ungracefully at his sides to convince him. Drum returned reluctantly to the shorter grass of the track along the side of the hill, and Holly's attention strayed out across Wigtown Bay. She watched seagulls dip flashily over the quiet water. The bold edges of the Galloway hills rose above the other shore. She felt a surge of happiness rising in her chest.

She reached down and patted Drum's neck again to express her feelings, and he nodded into a trot. She leaned forward eagerly.

"Go, boy, go!" she urged, and he broke into his springy canter.

Holly felt her grin broaden even as she grabbed the front of the saddle for extra support.

The air whipped past her, and she never even saw the nesting female pheasant hurtle upwards, feeling only Drum's startled swerve, and her feet come up out of the stirrups. The grass turned sideways, rushed towards her and the earth knocked out her breath.

Drum sidestepped Holly neatly, and paused. She lay gasping on the grass and saw him toss his head, twitching the reins out of her hand before she realised. Then he turned decisively around, his too-short, jaunty tail swinging as he stepped away from her.

Her chest heaved and her breath came in painful jolts as she struggled slowly to her knees. She put out her hands on the cool grass, and pushed herself to her feet.

Where would he go? What if she lost him? What could she say to Liddy? Or wouldn't he just go straight home, telling the whole world that she had fallen off and let go of him?

She straightened up painfully, and then set off after the straying pony. He had gone through an open gate into the next field, which was backed by a small wood.

Drum no longer looked so confident, she was pleased to see. He hesitated now, at the woodland edge, his little ears flickering. Holly ran, and very nearly caught up with him, stumbling, feeling very low to earth after being in the saddle.

"Drum!" she called.

But then she saw him make up his mind, drop his nose and forge through a thicket of hawthorn and wild roses on his way into the wood.

Breathless, she ran again, and then pushed her way after him. A hawthorn branch scraped her arm painfully. She could just see his coarse black tail ahead as he squeezed through a further narrow gap in a rough fence of hazel hurdles.

She heard him whicker softly as he stepped forwards, and then she was at the hurdles herself, losing sight of him in the thickets. Tripping over roots and long brambles, she stumbled between the hurdles, half blinded by the sudden shade inside the wood.

As her eyes adjusted to the green light, she saw that Drum was safely caught, held now by a middle-aged woman.

Holly sighed with relief.

"Thank you!" she called.

The woman said nothing. Holly noticed the woman was really staring at her, as though trying to fix everything about her in her memory.

It was embarrassing. Holly glared back.

"She looks well odd herself" she thought.

The woman wore at least two layers of brown skirts, which came down to her ankles. Around her shoulders she had a long thick cloth like a rug, over a rather grubby white blouse. Her hair was gathered back in an untidy bun. The strong hands holding onto Drum were rather dirty.

Without speaking to Holly, the woman turned her attention to the pony, stroking his nose. She nodded at him and straightened his shaggy forelock.

"Welcome back again, wee one", Holly heard her say to the pony's quiet eye. Drum stood like a statue.

Holly stared.

The woman was as brown as the woods. She looked strong, and though the lines on her face were pleasant, she was not smiling.

Holly dropped her eyes uncomfortably, and then looked around her.

She was standing in a woodland clearing, large enough for the sun to reach in to nourish carefully tended beds of herbs and vegetables. A low kind of tent, just cloths stretched over bent saplings really, stood in a patch of sunlight, backed by birch trees. Smoke drifted from a fire in front of it.

Drum shifted, hoping to graze.

Holly took a deep breath.

"I'm really sorry. Thanks for catching him."

She stepped forward to take the reins. To her surprise and alarm the woman tightened her hold on Drum and forced the reluctant pony to step back.

"What fetched ye here lassie?" The woman's eyes were green, and very piercing. Her Scots accent was much stronger than Liddy and Callum's.

"I fell off, and he," she pointed to Drum "he went through your fence, so I followed him. I hope he hasn't broken it," she added cautiously.

The woman continued to watch her.

"This yin, is he your galloway?" She lifted one hand from the reins and caressed Drum's neck. The pony swung his muzzle towards her, and his nostrils fluttered with appreciation.

"He's very like to a pony I had, years back", said the woman more softly, not waiting for Holly to answer. She looked up at Holly and smiled. Her face was transformed by it.

Holly grasped that damage to fences and property was not a problem. She stepped forward, putting out her own hand to stroke Drum's nose, and this time the woman did not make him move back.

"He's called Drum", Holly volunteered.

"Aye, and a good name for him too," said the woman. "What about yours?"

"I'm Holly. Holly Berry."

Holly noticed the woman did not react at all to her name, she merely nodded. "Then good day to ye Holly. I am Hawthorne Agnew."

Drum followed Hawthorne Agnew on a loose rein, docile and obedient. She led the way past the tent thing. Behind it was a pen made from more hurdles, with water in a wooden bucket. Hawthorne Agnew opened a gap and Drum stepped quietly through. Fumbling a little with the straps as though they weren't quite familiar, Hawthorne Agnew took off his saddle and bridle and laid them in the grass, propped carefully against the outside of the hurdle pen. Drum began to graze.

Holly wondered briefly whether she was safe, and whether the brown woman would give her Drum back and let them leave.

"Ye'll take a bite to eat, lassie." Hawthorne Agnew was smiling again. She squatted by the fire. On the fire was a pot, propped at an angle and blackened by flames. It was steaming.

A delicious smell of meaty stew caused Holly sudden pangs of hunger. "Rabbit" said Hawthorne, and she used a ladle to scoop out two bowlfuls of the rich, velvety meat and vegetables. She sat down on a large log near the fire, and motioned to Holly to sit beside her.

Holly's attention was on the ladle. "Is that made of – bone?"

Hawthorne Agnew laughed. "Nay lass, it's horn."

She looked at Holly.

"You've travelled, haven't ye Holly?"

At the word, Holly felt the hair rise on the back of her neck. Part of her tried to respond briskly ("Of course I've travelled, I've been to France, and Italy). But the absolute strangeness of the word when Hawthorne used it transfixed her, obliterating passports, planes and euros.

41

"You and yon galloway," Hawthorne commented, and passed Holly another, much smaller horn spoon. She picked up her own spoon, but did not dip it into her bowl.

"He brought ye. Ye know that, dinna ye?"

"I don't know anything!" Holly cried out in panic.

Hawthorne's face softened. "It's nae a problem Holly. I mean you've travelled along some years, not just through some old hurdles. And the galloway, he's been before."

"Do you mean Drum?"

Hawthorne's eyes looked patiently at Holly. "Aye, the galloway." She gestured in the direction of Drum's pen.

"I know him. He knows me. He's worked these woods before."

Holly could make nothing of this. She dipped her spoon into her bowl. The stew tasted wonderful. A slim black cat, tall on his legs, came and sat by her feet, leaning warmly against her jeans.

Later, when the bowls of stew had gone, Holly followed Hawthorne around her garden. Hawthorne identified beds of tall angelica, with tiny foaming white flowers, then clumps of vivid blue borage, straggling lovage twice Holly's height and long grey-green undulations of lavender. Hawthorne made Holly rub her fingers gently on their leaves so the crushing intensified the smell.

"It's good medicine." Hawthorne rubbed a sprig of lavender in her brown hand. "There, Holly."

Holly became absorbed in the sweet, pungent scents of the plants, and the alternately rough, soft or needle-like

42

nature of their warm leaves. She bent forward into the green shade of the bed and with a reach, pinched off an attractive ferny leaf from a handsome blue green plant.

"Not that one." Hawthorne's voice was suddenly sharp. "Not all herbs are kind. That one is the Monkshood, and he can kill. Come, wash yer hands."

Impressed, and a little alarmed, Holly dabbled her fingers in a bucket of greenish water.

Hawthorne was gathering up the bridle for Drum. "Help me lass, I'm not as young as I used to be, and your Drum is as he ever was."

Drum watched them, showing a wily white of eye, and at Holly's approach he stepped sideways, lifting his head out of reach.

Hawthorne smiled broadly at Holly. Then she stepped purposefully forward, double-bluffed the pony so he was momentarily cornered, and deftly caught him, looping the reins quickly and quietly around his neck.

Holly managed to get the saddle safely back on, and between them they tightened the girth against Drum's bulging ribcage. The pony held his breath until Hawthorne nudged him off balance and heaved the strap tight. He let out a long resigned snort, shook his neck and mane, then snatched a good mouthful of grass before Holly could stop him.

"I like those. Can I smell those?" Holly, clutching the reins, managed to indicate a low growing clump of purple-blue flowering plants. Hawthorne followed her gesture, then raised her eyebrows. She bent, and without a word, picked a leaf and passed it to Holly.

"Ye can't stop water flowing" she remarked to the slim cat, which was washing itself in a patch of sunlight. Holly stared, distracted, and then crushed the leaf and sniffed.

"Clary" said Hawthorne. "Clary, for clear-eye. Helps with the seeing, lass."

The strong woody scent took Holly by surprise. It did seem to clear her head. She smiled at Hawthorne with a new-found confidence.

Hawthorne smiled back.

Holly grasped the reins and heaved herself up onto Drum, and Hawthorne led the pony back to the hurdles, pulled them aside and sent him through with a slap to his rump.

"Visit whenever you will," she heard Hawthorne's voice over the muffled thud of Drum's hooves on the grass.

"Yes, I will! Thanks Hawthorne," Holly called, and turned to look back over her shoulder.

She pulled the pony up and turned him round.

The hurdles had gone, and in their place was a thick green hawthorn hedge, with flowering honeysuckle winding through it.

# 7    Late

Drum's untidy mane bobbed on either side of his neck to the rhythm of his trot as Holly steered him homewards. She rode him automatically, as she tried to fathom what had just happened. Perhaps she had met a gypsy.

She tried to remember if there were still gypsies living in tents in the woods of Britain in the twenty first century. Didn't they have camper vans now? Travellers. The brown woman – Hawthorne - had said "travelling". Holly remembered her flash of understanding, at that word, of something instinctive, something recognised.    And something uneasy. She pushed the memory away.

She turned Drum onto the shore road and the pony's shod hooves rang reassuringly on the tarmac as he improved his pace, homeward bound.    Holly thought about how Hawthorne handled Drum.    She was very good at it. Or Drum had been very good for Hawthorne. (Why?)

There were two boys on bikes waiting by the gate to the paddock.    Heart sinking, Holly saw it was Callum and his friend Will, recognisable by his red curls.    Drum dropped back into a walk of his own accord and halted by the gate.

"Liddy's about to ring the police" said Callum casually as they arrived. He turned away and kicked his pedal up to set off.

"What?  Callum – wait," Holly slid anxiously down from the saddle, stretching out a hand to bar his way. "Callum, Liddy's what?"

"Yeah, Scotland's Book Town Tragedy.  City Girl Carried Away By Water Horse" added Will with relish.

"What are you on about?"

"Come on Will" said Callum.  "Just when I was getting used to her not being around, too."  He stepped down heavily on his pedal and rode off.

Will looked after him, then back at Holly.

"Where were you anyway?  Haven't you been back to Good Garden Books yet?  His freckled face was puzzled, and a little concerned.  "Liddy was getting really worried."

Holly just stared at him.

Will shook his red ringlets out of his eyes, shrugged, and rode off after Callum.


A nasty thought struck her.  She snatched her sleeve back to see her watch.  She had only just had lunch with Hawthorne, right?

Her watch said the time was now ten to six in the evening.

She had been gone all day.


Rushing, she unsaddled Drum, shooed him into the field, dragged her own bike out of the hedge and pedalled madly back up into Wigtown.  The saddle lay awkwardly across the handlebars, unbalancing her, and she was laden with her backpack, stuffed with bridle and helmet.  Panting

46

and hot, but anxious to get back before Callum and Will had had too much time to talk to Liddy, Holly struggled up past the County Buildings and slid off the bike by Good Garden Books.

She leaned the bike and saddle against the wall, and bent down for a moment to gasp for breath. Then she shook her sticky hair out of her eyes and hurried in through the open front door.

"Sorry" she said to a customer she jostled in the hall. The man moved unwillingly out of her way, and craning round his arm she spotted Liddy in the Gardening History Room next to the Grete Herball's glass case.

"Liddy, Liddy – I'm back!"

Liddy swung round. Her hand flew to her mouth, and her eyes were round and strained.

"Holly – where have you been? It's so late. I've been so worried, what would I say to Stan – I thought -" she let out what might have been almost a sob, and stepped forward – "Oh Holly!"

Holly found herself caught in an unexpected embrace. She stiffened, and Liddy let go suddenly.

"Sorry" they said together.

Holly smiled feebly.

Liddy frowned.

She pointed out how irresponsible it was of Holly to go off without telling anyone where she was for hours on end. And how it wasn't fair to take an elderly pony off riding all day. Had he had any rests, anything to drink or eat?

47

Holly opened her mouth to explain, but then gave up. She confirmed, not looking at Liddy, that Drum had enjoyed rest, grazing and water.

Liddy went over it all over again, and Holly hung her head. Eventually Liddy paused for breath.

"Have you had anything to eat or drink?"

"Well, not since lunch" said Holly truthfully. "I don't feel that hungry though." The delicious stew had only been an hour ago, after all.

"You must be famished", said Liddy firmly, "I've got a big lamb stew on the go. Twenty minutes."

"Oh. Good," Holly managed.


Later, it occurred to her that Callum and Will had only returned to the house as the big lamb stew was served. They sat next to one another and did not speak to Holly.

They had not bothered to rush back to Good Garden Books to tell Liddy that she was safe, after all.

# 8    Her Red

*It is too cold to sleep. In the attics under the sarking in the roof she has not enough bedding to keep out the frost. She shivers with cold under a threadbare coverlet, although she has thought to put on all the clothes she owns before lying down. She does not find the ancient mattress lumpy and itchy with its straw filling, but the intense cold is misery.*

*She lies on her side, curled into a ball, winding her Red round and round her hands. Her Red was once perhaps a scarf, a woollen length, now so thinned and matted it is hard to guess what it might have been. Even its colour is unclear, but she has always thought of it as her Red, so red it must have been.*

*Through and round, through and round her fingers goes the Red.*

*The Red helps to keep away the Darkment.*

*When she comes to the last finger, the Mark, she winds the Red around and around it, obscuring it from her view, as if the Red (always on her side) could unmake it and leave her whole, with five fingers on her left hand, as there are on her right.*

# 9 In The Year of Mister Wormelow's Lord

Hope u r being gd 4 Liddy. Miss u v much. V boring without u.
Sorry w end visit p poned. Will ring Sat, Dad xxx

For the next few days Holly was cautious. She wondered whether Liddy had told Stan about her not coming home all day. It was up to her not to cause any trouble between them. She did not want to fall out with Liddy.

Fortunately, Liddy continued to be cheerful and friendly, and indeed behaved the day after Holly's escapade as though nothing had happened. Which made everything easier, except she really did want to visit Hawthorne again.

Callum was another matter. It seemed as if she'd fallen out with Callum without even trying to. So far as she could see, he avoided her. If she came into the kitchen, he left through the conservatory. She felt a bit sorry for Liddy, because Callum was often grumpy and difficult with her. Though at least he would stay in the same room as his mother.

The days passed slowly that week. Holly's moods swung between excitement and frustration. She tried to act unconcerned. She had never tried so hard to hide anything. Something out of the ordinary had happened to her at last, and the more she thought about it, the more curious and intrigued she was. She had "travelled". (She wished she knew more history). When (and actually where) did Hawthorne live? She began to plan ahead for her next trip to Hawthorne's wood. If the problem was getting back in time for lunch, then she wouldn't come back.

The next two days offered no opportunity, first because of a stint of helping in the shop, which was tactical, befriend Liddy, and then due to torrential rain. On the third morning however, Holly could tell even from her bed that the day was more promising, and she had, with careful forethought, gained permission to take Drum out for a "picnic". This would get her out of returning for lunch, in case she had trouble with the time again.

She was faintly uneasy about the time thing. In all the stories she knew or had read where time travel took place, no real time was ever consumed by the experience. This was clearly much more convenient. And what if she missed by more than a few hours? A week? A decade? (Centuries?)

Pushing away the thought, Holly climbed out of bed, dressed quickly and went to look out of her window. She pushed the dull brass catch in the middle of the window frame and heaved up the sash with a loud rattle. She leaned out.

Early morning air filtered refreshingly into the room. She rested her elbows on the sill and gazed down the length of the Main Street.

Wigtown was lit by the first sunshine of the day, and was so quiet Holly was aware of birdsong. She caught a faint smell of mown grass mingled with cooking smells from the butcher's, and running behind that was the salty smell of the marshes down at Wigtown Bay. White gulls wheeled over the old slate roofs, catching the light and calling raucously. It was a good day for a picnic.

Making sandwiches in the kitchen with Liddy, Holly thought to ask,

"Where's Callum? Is he up yet?"

Liddy sighed briefly. "I think so."

Holly gave her a straight look. "Is he avoiding me Liddy?"

"Have to say it looks that way." Liddy was terse. Then she added, "Not your fault though Holly."

"Well it's not really yours either." Holly met Liddy's eyes quickly, then looked away.

Liddy sounded a bit overcome. "Thanks Holly," she said, and rushed across the kitchen to get a slice of cake for Holly's picnic lunch.

Scrambling up onto Drum with some difficulty due to the backpack laden with picnic lunch, Holly was impatient to reach the wood where she had found Hawthorne Agnew. Drum, surprised at her purposeful attitude, set off quite smartly on the way out of Wigtown, and even trotted willingly along the track by the shore. However his pace lagged as he approached the path through the field that bounded the wood. He dropped back to a walk and snatched at some long grass.

Holly pressed him forward firmly, struck by the thought that she could reach Hawthorne more quickly by the gate across the track at the near end of the wood. "After all", she said to Drum, "I'm sure you don't need to go to the trouble of dumping me and running off round the other side every time we go near this place."

Drum's ears flickered. They jogged steadily to the gate and pulled up. Holly stared into the wood. The track curved away on the other side of the gate between young birch trees. Suddenly doubtful, Holly nonetheless slid off, unfastened the gate and led Drum through. He followed, looking deeply bored, and when she lifted her foot to the stirrup to remount he circled unhelpfully away from her. She hopped after him, lurched aboard and clung as he set off at a trot. But as they rounded the bend in the track, she saw the conifers. Densely planted behind a thin screen of birch, they filled the whole wood. Her track just stopped: there was no way through. Drum yanked on the reins, stretched his neck and snatched grass.

Holly's disappointment was bitter. She turned him and rode slowly back to the gate, dismounted and led him through. Climbing back on by letting him graze was more successful, if not by the book. Settling herself in the saddle, she heaved his head up again and hesitated.

Drum set off at a plodding walk. Fed up, Holly let him. He trundled round the edge of the wood. Suddenly, she began to hope he knew where he was going. She let the reins go loose on his neck. He walked steadily on, and then put his head down and grazed. Holly fought her frustration, and sat still. Drum munched appreciatively. He took a step forward, then one sideways, apparently to eat a particularly pleasing patch of red clover. Holly felt tears of frustration and disappointment trying to rise in her chest.

Drum raised his head a few inches, chewed, and then stepped towards the wood. Holly held her breath, and then yelped as he pushed through the tearing twigs of a particularly painful bush. As he forged through she saw the hurdles, sagging gently as ever in the warm sunshine. Just in time, she ducked low on his withers as he scrambled through the gap, feeling branches whip just above her head and catch at her backpack.


As she sat up again cautiously, she heard Drum whicker a greeting. He had seen Hawthorne Agnew by her tent, and to Holly's intense, sweeping relief, she saw that Hawthorne was pleased to see them.

"You're well come, young Holly" she said as Drum approached. "I can use your help today."

"Oh" said Holly. "I mean, hello Hawthorne. How can I – what do we have to do?"

Hawthorne was patting Drum. "As clever as a cat", she said to him. Drum blew loudly through his nostrils and shoved at her skirts with his nose. Then Hawthorne looked at Holly, her brown face creased with amusement.

"I have a paying job to do" she said. "I don't much need for shillings, but I like to lay a bit aside for winter. T'is the minister, Mister Wormelow. He has need of a whole new manse, and so he has need of a well, and so has need of me."

Deeply puzzled, Holly followed Hawthorne back to the tent built on curved-over saplings. Hawthorne motioned Holly to wait outside while she crawled in, reappearing with bundles of cloth over one arm. When Hawthorne had stood up again, the cloths became identified as a long brown tweed skirt, patched in a couple of places, and a thick flannel shirt.

"You'd best put these on." Hawthorne suggested. "Else the minister'll be having a few words to say."

"And he's not a man with only a few words" she added.

When Holly had changed her clothes Hawthorne looked at her critically, then wound another piece of cloth about her head, mostly covering her hair.

"You'll do" she said. "Good job those boots is so dirty."

Hawthorne turned her attention to Drum, stripping him of his saddle and bridle. She slipped a worn rope halter over his head, ferreted in the back of the tent, and heaved out a pad with a girth, onto which she attached two large woven baskets. Drum bore all this with unusual patience, Holly noticed.

"He may's well work, as he's here" said Hawthorne. She unwrapped a large bundle, showed Holly carved clothes pegs, then a smaller bundle of horn spoons like the one Holly remembered from her first visit.

"Do you make these?" Holly asked.

55

"I do, and my mother and grandmother before me." Hawthorne spoke proudly, and her eyes flashed a smile.

Holly wondered again about exactly *when* she had "travelled" to. Vikings? Victorians?

"Hawthorne," she began, "when is it? I mean, what year is this? And where am I?"

Hawthorne smiled at her. "'T'is the year of Mister Wormelow's Lord, seventeen hundred and ninety six, in the parish of Wigtown, in the county of Wigtownshire."

Holly stroked a horn spoon in wonder. "I come from the year two thousand and twelve" she said. It was like being in a film. "And I'm from Carlisle. But I'm staying in Wigtown."

"My, my" said Hawthorne gently.

She added a last bundle which had sticks poking out of it onto the top of one of Drum's panniers, and then they set off, leaving the clearing along a winding green path. Holly recognised nothing until they rounded the edge of a hill and she saw Wigtown Bay gleaming silver at the horizon. To her left a cluster of houses clung together on top of the hill. There were much fewer of them than she was used to seeing.

"So it is still Wigtown?" she said to Hawthorne, who was walking by Drum's head, holding the halter rope.

"Indeed."

"Aren't you curious Hawthorne, about where I come from? What it's like now? I mean, in my time?"

Hawthorne looked down at her, faintly puzzled. "I don't need to ask that Holly."

Holly went quiet. Hawthorne was not altogether easy to talk to. She seemed so unsurprised by the strangeness of the situation that Holly felt a bit rebuffed. She wished she could tell someone who would appreciate the weirdness of everything. Even, she almost wished she could tell Callum. And why did Drum do everything Hawthorne told him to?

For a few minutes they walked in silence, except for birdsong. Holly became aware of the lack of distant traffic noise. She thought, no plane has ever yet shrieked across this sky. The lane was roughly stone surfaced here, and Drum's shod hooves rang on cobbles and thudded on earth. Her long skirt swished very quietly. One of Hawthorne's boots creaked sometimes.

"Here we are lass."

The lane had brought them to the very edge of Wigtown. Hawthorne steadied Drum and turned him into a gateway. A fine sandstone villa gleamed, new quarried and stark. Around it was a building site mess of discarded beam ends, sawdust piles, buckets sludged with half-dried paint, lumps of stone and wood, flattened grass and sprouting weeds.

A plump, bothered-looking man dressed in black with a plain white collar scurried towards them. The Minister, Holly supposed.

"Good morning Mistress Agnew, I hope you keep well?" He bowed a little over his hands. His small eyes met

Hawthorne's gaze for a moment and then bobbed busily away again.

"Come this way, come this way. They tell me there should be water under the earth on this side of the grounds, but you'll know best, of course."

They followed him along the side of the new manse. He ignored Holly completely.

Hawthorne tethered Drum to a surviving apple branch. She turned to look at the man.

"We'll get to work now minister. I work best when I'm not watched."

"Of course, of course."

He really was most uncomfortable, Holly decided. He bowed again, then turned and threaded his way through the builders' debris to disappear back into his house.


Hawthorne watched him go. Then she began to unpack the bundle of sticks from Drum's baskets.

"What are we – what are you going to do?" asked Holly.

Hawthorne was unwrapping cloth from around her bundle. She knelt to do this, and smiled suddenly up at Holly.

"Do ye not know what these are Holly? See – these are my divining sticks. They find water when I hold them. They will find water when ye hold them too, I'll be bound!"

She showed Holly how to hold one of the forked sticks, the backs of her hands to the earth, her thumbs braced on the springy ends. Then Hawthorne took one herself and led Holly at a slow walk across the rough grass.

58

They were a little distance apart but side by side, when Holly's stick, without any warning, twisted up in her hands so sharply that she lost hold of it and squealed in surprise. Hawthorne was laughing, she seemed pleased.

"There, that didnae take long Holly, you've a talent. Now let's be trying a line from where ye are."

Gradually, with Hawthorne's help, Holly began to see that they were plotting a line where water flowed below the surface. Hawthorne could tell from faint variations where the strongest pull was, and the deepest source of water.

"Fetch me that white stone Holly."

And the spot for the new well was marked.

They knocked on the door of the manse. When the minister answered, he stepped quickly out, closing the door protectively behind him. He held a plain black bible.

"There's water below the white stone," Hawthorne said. "It's deep and strong. You and yours will not run out."

"Thank you Mistress Agnew. Was it two shillings we agreed?" He was counting out the money as he spoke. He seemed in a great hurry for them to leave, Holly thought.

And at her thought, he looked at her suddenly, his glance stopping at the forked stick still in her hands. His right hand lifted urgently to hold up the bible between himself and her.

He kept it there with one hand while he tipped the money into Hawthorne's outstretched palm.

"Thank you minister." Hawthorne's voice was cold.

She turned back towards Drum and the gateway. Behind her, Holly heard the new manse door open and swiftly shut as Mister Wormelow retreated.

Holly was indignant. "What was wrong with him? Aren't we good enough?"

Hawthorne untied Drum and walked steadily through the gateway before she answered.

"Well, no lass. He disnae think we're good enough and that's a fact. He's a man of the cloth, and I'm a tinkler. He even thinks you're a tinkler." Her brown face creased with amusement, then darkened a little.

"You mean like a tinker? Like a gypsy?" queried Holly.

Hawthorne looked calmly at her. "If you like. Tinkler is our word for it. Here."

She paused, and then went on: "The Minister Wormelow is feared of the divining sticks. For him, that's earth magic, even witchcraft, and none of the Good Book. But his lady wife hears that that way she'll get her deep well by her new house, and so today they had a need of me."

She brightened suddenly. "Still, I have me my two shillings. And there's much worse than the Minister Wormelow in this town to worry about."

Holly smiled broadly at her, and expressed her feelings by patting Drum firmly on the neck. The pony sighed, and snatched a mouthful of grass.

Back in the green shade of Hawthorne's wood, they let Drum graze, and Holly shared her picnic with Hawthorne.

"What strange taste is this?!" Hawthorne pulled a face.
"Er, Marmite, Hawthorne".

By the end of the picnic Holly had learned to call the tent a bender and drink a tisane made with the hot water brewed on the tripod poured over lemon balm leaves from the herb garden. She had also taken charge of her own hazel divining stick.

"The hazel's just springy enough, see," Hawthorne explained, "and it's a tree as likes water, so ye cannae go wrong."

Promising to practice with the divining stick, Holly shed her skirt and shirt and re-saddled Drum. Calling out her goodbyes, she rode back through the sagging hazel hurdles into her own century.

# 10  This Doesn't Work

Holly stepped out through the pleasant shade of the conservatory, a vine leaf brushing her shoulder as she made for the garden door. She held the divining stick Hawthorne had given her carefully in one hand. Outside, the heat of the afternoon poured heavily over her as she made her way up the path.

Once on the patch of grass near the end of the garden Holly took hold, just as she'd been shown, of her dowsing twig. Concentrating, she began to work her way along an imaginary line across the width of the garden. She stepped forwards, two steps, then three. Nothing.

She took two steps forward, up the length of the garden, and then turned and set off again, across its width. One. Two. Three steps.

The twig vibrated under her fingers, once, then stilled.

Elation rose in her. She turned and began to work her way back to pick up the vibration again.

"Oh come on!"

Callum's voice broke in upon her concentration like glass shattering.

"What're you looking for in our garden anyway?"

He had come out of the conservatory and was standing lower down the path, glaring at her.

"I'm not *looking* for anything," said Holly coldly.

"Is it treasure hunting? Or are you one of those new age hippies?"

She sensed that Callum had suddenly let go his restraint of the last few weeks. She held the twig, and waited.

He drove his hands into his pockets and glowered at her.

"Even berks with metal detectors are supposed to ask if anyone *minds* them pilfering off land that doesn't belong to them."

"Don't be so stupid. I'm not looking for treasure!" Holly's voice rose, shocked at the intensity of the interruption. She could not stop herself. (She didn't want to).

"Why are you so touchy Callum? You never bother to speak to me for weeks and then come and yell at me about metal detectors!"

"Yell?" said Callum coldly. "Who's doing the yelling? I can see it must be embarrassing though, found playing at finding stuff with a hippy stick."

"Don't act more stupid than you are. This is a divining stick and it works. You don't know what you're talking about. Any more than you understand other people's points of view. You're rude to me, and selfish to Liddy and Stan."

Callum's face went still. Then he stepped forward and without warning wrenched the twig out of Holly's hands. She let out a gasp and tried to grab it back.

"Right, let's see if it works," Callum said. He moved quickly out of Holly's reach, held out the twig and took a step. "Yes, yes, I'm getting something, the hippy stick is twitching..."

He stopped, and held up the twig, above his head and away from Holly.

"You know you need to get a grip Holly. This doesn't work. And Liddy and Stan doesn't work. My ma's going to be sick to death of him by Christmas. Then you'll have to move out."

Something about the certainty in his voice enraged Holly beyond all bearing. Furious, beside herself, she launched herself at Callum, taking him by surprise. In an instant she had knocked hard against him, torn the divining stick back out of his hand, and set off at a run towards the pend gate at the end of the garden.

She was sobbing with anger, and now she gripped the stick in both hands, feeling the faint comfort of her thumbs curving over its ends as she ran, wanting only to get out of the garden (and then Callum could explain to Liddy why she wasn't there).

She was only a couple of strides from the gate when the twig reacted, bending itself almost double in her hands. She cried out and staggered to a halt, staring.

The wall, and the garden gate, had gone.

Another gate, this one unpainted, the wood weathered to a pale grey, stood partly open in front of her. The sound of clopping hooves on cobbles filled her ears, and she saw a horse wearing cart harness passing the gate opening, led by a man who had just gone out of sight. She just glimpsed his back, and his hand on the horse's bridle.

"'S'all right Tam! I've got old Wormelow's nag here now. Just wait on."

Holly dropped the dowsing stick.

The twenty-first century wall and gate were back.

They looked entirely solid.

A butterfly meandered slowly past and settled against the sunbaked stone.

Callum was beside her, and now he was staring not at the wall but at her. She gazed back at him, too shocked to speak.

Then she bent and picked up the divining stick protectively. Callum still did not move, or take his eyes off her.

"And what in *heck* was that?" he said accusingly.

"I dunno" said Holly, keeping her face as blank as she could. She could feel her heart beating far too fast.

"OK", said Callum, "OK. I admit something did happen. Did you know it was going to?" He sounded faintly alarmed now.

Holly looked at him intently. He looked really worried, which made her feel better.

She said, "No. I didn't".

She raised her chin. "But now you know. It does - work."

"I thought divining was just to find water." Callum let out a sudden snort of shocked laughter. "Not shift masonry and magic up horses!"

Holly glared at him without speaking.

"Ok, ok." He looked quickly down. "Sorry. Alright? But did you see that too?"

Holly nodded slowly.

Callum looked back at her, and then, as though he'd made up his mind about something, shook his head and shrugged.

"This is way weird," he said.


He turned away from her and walked back down the path to the house, disappearing from view into the conservatory.

Holly scowled after him.

"Prat," she said, out loud in the empty garden.

# 11   The Knack of Taming Bears

*She presses herself quickly back against the whitewashed wall as Mr Wormelow's chestnut clatters down the pend, the men shouting and hurrying. They take no notice of her, but she turns her eyes down to be sure of attracting no attention.*

*Hastily she empties the cold dirty water from the slops bucket into the gutter, and turns back towards the rear of the house. Already Lizzy is calling. She hurries to lift the kitchen latch.*

*"Where have you been Sparrow?" Lizzy doesn't look round from her task. Her hands work swiftly, chopping carrots with rhythmic thuds on the scrubbed table.*

*"You know we're behindhand today already. You don't want to make him angry do you now?"*

*"No Lizzy" she says, and busies herself to tend the fire in the range. She doesn't know Lizzy very well. Doctor Sliddery cannot keep a servant in The Crow House, they whisper, in town. Lizzy is another in a long line of cooks who come in to do.*

*"You're a funny solemn wee thing" Lizzy scoops the carrots into the stock pot and wipes her hands on her apron. She straightens up painfully, her hands in her back, surveying Sparrow.*

*"Is it true what they say about you? That you came from no home?" Lizzy seems to like to talk.*

"I don't know" Sparrow says. She looks up. Lizzy's face looks suddenly gentle. Sparrow studies her silently. Then she offers a little more. "I was only a wee bairn, not four years old. But I mind I had me a mother."

Lizzy says nothing, but her eyes have softened. The silence stretches.

Sparrow stares at the kitchen flags. She whispers.

"I mind her holding me."

Then she looks up, very quickly, and down again.

"But Doctor Sliddery says he took me in. He says she wanted rid". Her voice drifts down.

"Ah, that." Lizzy steals a swift glance at Sparrow's left hand, and crosses herself. "I wonder."

She rubs at an eye with the back of her hand, mindful of her onion stained fingers.

"The good doctor knows a bargain though. We neither of us costs him a fair price but still he has his every comfort in this house. An old body told me a story the ither day."

Sparrow looks carefully into Lizzy's face, reddened and shiny with her work in the kitchen. She reads a sort of kindness in the older woman's eyes, mingled with the more hardened need to survive.

"This old body, she tellt me them tinklers with the bear, them that they say came out of Hungary, they lost a bairn. Didn't say how long ago, mind. Now then, our Sparrow – maybe you're a tinkler's bairn! Maybe you got the knack of taming bears!" Lizzy laughs loudly.

68

*Behind her a sudden hiss and spitting as a pan boils over takes her rushing away to the range.*

*The distant ringing of a bell causes Sparrow to freeze, then run hurriedly from the kitchen in the direction of the study.*

# 12   "Process againft overmanie years of age..."

"I gotta go Will," Callum said, downing the last of a can of Irn Bru, "I'm helping in the shop this afternoon.  Dusting duty for everyone.  You could help me and I'd get out sooner".

"Sorry."  Will swallowed the last of his sandwich and shook his head.  His red curls quivered energetically.  "We can get online at two o'clock, at Duncan's.  If you get done in time why not come along?"


Callum trudged out of Will's house and along through the West Port towards North Main Street.

He mused gloomily on life.  He got to do dusting old books with a completely unwanted would-be step-sister, while Duncan squeezed in on his friendship with Will.  He got to live in a creepy house with a ghost in a book, and a mad unwanted would-be step-sister who thought he was just a kid.  The bloke in the book was seriously unpleasant.  You could just tell.  Callum didn't like to think too much about him – Doctor Jared Sliddery.  He didn't like to think about how he'd lived in the house.  Which room had he slept in?  Worse, which room had he died in?

Callum stuck his hands in his pockets as he walked, and glowered at the stone flags.  If he lived in a book he'd be able to tell his friends about the ghost in the Grete Herball, but in real life he reckoned they'd probably just think he'd lost his last remaining marble. Briefly he considered (not for the first time) telling Liddy. How come she'd never met the spook, the time she'd spent poring over that volume?

And what was he supposed to do about Holly? That stunt she pulled with the dowsing stick-twig-thing. "If that's real too, then we are in the shit Callum" he addressed himself out loud.

Then he looked furtively back down the pavement to make sure no-one had heard him. Particularly no-one he knew.


He heard Liddy laughing and bantering with a customer in the café as he came in, so he paused in the doorway of the Gardening History Room. It was empty. The Grete Herball lay peacefully in its glass case. Callum backed out again and went to find his mother and his duster.


Stepping round an intent and silent book browser to dust a low shelf some time later, Callum heard Liddy calling him and wandered out into the hallway.

"There you are Callum. Alison's come in now, so Holly and I are going for a wander down to the harbour, get some fresh air to counteract the effects of Old Volume Disease. Want to come?"

Callum noticed she said this brightly, and as though she hadn't thought it out extremely carefully.

"No," he said with satisfaction. "Will and Duncan want me to go back. Duncan's found some new game."

When they had gone, Callum plodded up to his room. He had decided to tell Will about the spook, but not if Duncan was there too. Which meant not today.

It was as he went back downstairs that he had an idea. It would be a safe (well, safeish) way to see if the spook was, well, real.

"Checking on my own head now," he thought wryly. He dumped his hoodie on the bottom of the stairs, and looked down the hall.

The bookshop was quiet, and no-one was in the Gardening History Room at all. He went in, then shut the door after him. He got the key out of the table drawer, and unlocked the glass case.

He hesitated. Still no-one around. (Alison tended to stay in the café, nose in book until asked to do otherwise).

Slowly he lifted the glass lid back, and then opened the Grete Herball. He breathed in its leathery, musty reek. He checked again that the door was shut, and that no-one seemed to be about to come in.

He can't see me. I know he can't see me. But I can see him. Callum felt his heart speeding up.

Just don't talk to yourself Callum, and you'll be fine. Sit tight and find out what he's up to. You'll be fine. Just a bit stuck till he leaves the room, that's all.

He turned the old pages, passing woodcuts and ornate headings until he was about three quarters of the way through the book. Then the page was under his hand, with the tables covered in jars and herbs.

"Be on your guard gentil reader…"

72

Bloody well will, thought Callum.

He took a deep breath and looked into the man's face. How could he ever have thought it looked kind? For a moment the heavy black lines of the woodcut took on their own pattern: the curve of jaw, the lines around eyes, the harsh lines by his mouth.

Then, as before, that tilting moment when the book became the room, and for a moment his head swam, and then the room surrounded him.

Callum took care to remain very still.

With only a miniscule movement of his head he looked down at his trainers on the oak floor, then moved, he reckoned, only his eyes to look at the man.

Who was staring back at him.

Callum's breath caught in his throat.

The man's eyes were very still. They seemed trained on Callum's face. Then he half-shrugged, and looked down again at his desk.

Very, very slowly, Callum let himself breathe.

No chopping herbs this time, Doctor Sliddery was writing. Callum watched him smooth the handsome length of a stiff black feather quill while he considered. Then he stretched out and dipped the nib in a silver-embossed inkwell and began to write. The nib scratched on the paper, but the sound was smooth and rhythmic. The house was very quiet.

"No traffic noise," thought Callum, still keeping perfectly still, and then revised this as a farm wagon rumbled past the window. He could see the horse's ears going by, but where he expected to make out the line of South Main Street opposite, all he could see were tall trees. As he watched, a crow glided heavily down onto the street. It strutted on the cobbles for a moment, then jumped and flapped out of sight.

"Bit of effort and I could date this," he thought. Keeping his feet still, he studied the room. It was recognisably the Gardening History Room: the tall folded window shutters were there, and the fireplace was indeed, as he remembered Liddy saying with enthusiasm, "an original". Funny to be able to verify that. On the shiny oak floor, between the desk where Doctor Sliddery was writing and the marble fireplace, lay a thick, richly coloured wool rug.

Doctor Sliddery made a sharp exclamation of impatience. Callum stiffened, but remained still as Doctor Sliddery reached out and rang a handbell that stood on his desk.

The sudden loudness of its peal jolted through Callum's body and he had to struggle not to move, but luckily the man's attention was now on the door. The fingers of one long white hand tapped irritably on the desk.

The door began to open, slowly and with care, and a child slid round it. But she was not like any child Callum had ever met. She was small, and looked extremely thin. Her clothes were shiny with wear and hung large on her. He had an impression of large dark eyes, lots of dark hair pulled back and tied behind her, and a small, pointy-chinned face. The other thing he noticed, couldn't help but notice, was that she was very frightened.

"Doctor Sliddery, sir," she said, and bobbed a kind of curtsey.

"My second quill." He was as cold as ice.

The girl scurried obediently across the room and opened a drawer in one of the tables laden with herbs. She took out another black quill, hastily closed the drawer again and presented it to the man seated at the desk, bobbing her head as she did so.

"In future, see to it you lay my desk correctly each morning girl. Another failure this week will see you punished. As you receive Christian charity in this house so must you work." On this last word Doctor Sliddery's hand slapped the table, and the girl shrank back towards the door.

Callum noticed that when you saw her side on, there was a strange streak of grey in her wiry hair where it was tied back above her ears. Then she fled round the door and was gone.

He envied her for having an excuse to leave.

Minutes ticked uncomfortably by.

Doctor Sliddery's quill pen scratched steadily. Callum began to ache from standing still. He thought of the café at home ("But this is home!") which was full of writers who moaned about the temptation of the fridge and the coffee pot when they were supposed to be writing. To Callum's increasing dismay the man he was watching seemed to have no such problems with concentration.

Time passed.

Doctor Sliddery worked on.

Callum willed him to need the loo.

At long last Doctor Sliddery placed a careful full stop and straightened his back. He looked at his work with unmistakeable satisfaction, laid down his quill and stood up. He looked straight through Callum, flexed his writing hand, then strode out of the room.

Callum executed a short dance of relief and triumph. Then he stepped towards the desk. The top sheet of paper, covered in a sloping hand, was difficult to read. Callum frowned. The first word at the top must be "against" –

"Process againft overmanie years of age, when Time be thine enemy. Do thou take a young childe, whose years are but few for this Process, yet onlye should thy Learning be surpaffing great."

There was a thunderous knocking noise.

Callum sprang away from the table, and froze.

The knocking came again, and with flooding relief, Callum realised the noise came from the street door, and not the door of Doctor Sliddery's study.

Callum seized his chance, and like last time, fled for the study door. Somebody was no doubt answering the door, and for all he knew would show the visitor into the study. He'd better get out before they came in.

He could hear voices.

He wondered, as his fingers closed round the doorknob that would let him out of the room, what he would do if Good Garden Books wasn't on the other side.

But then he was through, and it was.

Callum found himself apologising profusely to a customer whose toes happened to have been in the way of his return to the 21st century.

Embarrassed and disorientated, he scooped up the hoodie, then hesitated. Alison called out,

"Callum? Is that you?"

Callum made up his mind and went quickly out through the front door.


Outside the warm sunshine beamed dazzlingly back at him from the pavement. Callum slowly began to put some distance between himself and Doctor Sliddery's study. He walked slowly, watching the flagstones pass under his feet. His mind replayed Doctor Sliddery's cold eyes staring right through him.

There was way too much weird stuff going on.

"Hell's biscuits - a ghost. A really nasty ghost."

Realising he had muttered aloud, Callum glanced back over his shoulder. A couple of holiday makers emerged from Reading Lasses Café Bookshop, but luckily no-one he knew.

He was within sight of Duncan's house now. How could you just tell other people – normal people - about stuff like this?

He knew he wouldn't.

He stopped at Duncan's front door and raised his hand to the knocker. He wondered if Holly was thinking about the other stuff too.

Then the knocker fell, and Duncan's mum opened the door, and led him to Duncan's room, nattering on all the time about the long spell of fine weather or something.

# 13    Can You Keep a Secret?

Callum mooched in from the garden in search of shade, and ideally, relief from the unease he was carrying around with him about the author of The Grete Herball. He drifted through the kitchen and into the bookshop, making, without thinking about it, for the hall, which was always cool. (The Gardening History Room was even cooler, but no way was he going in there).

He slumped at the foot of the stairs, avoiding customers' eyes in case he had to say hello. An intense looking woman in sandals had paused close by him, but he relaxed when he saw she was just searching a bookcase, one finger out, working through the small but quirky Gardening Fiction section from N to T.

He could see a thin slice of the How To Room through the part open door. It looked quiet.

He heaved himself off the bottom step, went the long way round the intense woman without looking at her, and entered the room.

Too late to leave again unseen, he took in the sight of Holly, sitting cross-legged on the floor under the bookcase labelled, 'Herbs'. She looked round as he came in, and said, "Hi Callum," but not in a very friendly way.

"Hi," he said. He looked down at the floorboards, then up again.

Holly's glance flicked over him. She sighed.

"There are a lot of herb books," she said neutrally. "More than I thought. Oh for Google."

The internet had been down since the weekend. Callum looked down at the book she had open on the floor. There was a drawing of a leaf, then it went on about the properties of hazel. She saw him looking, and shut the book with a bang. Then she glared at him.

"All right," he said, totally fed-up. "Ok, I was out of order yesterday."

"Yeah," she said. "You were bloody rude." She stared him out. Then when he'd dropped his eyes her hostility towards him seemed to peter out.

"Oh, never mind." She was still scowling, but at a bookshelf, not him.

Callum felt faint guilt.

He shrugged.

"Well I never knew that stuff worked. And it was really weird. Sorry." He stared at the side of her face, half hidden with hanging down hair.

"You didn't know that might happen, did you?"

Holly jerked her head round and stared at him. Hard. What was up with her?

"Of course not," she said coldly. Then she sighed again and shook her head like she couldn't make her mind up.

"What?" he said.

To his surprise, Holly swivelled round on the floor, and leaned back on the bookcase, shoving the herb book to one side.

"Sit down," she said, "I've got to tell someone or I'll go nuts in this place."

Interested in spite of himself, Callum slid down and leaned on the bookcase opposite.

"Well, what?" he repeated.

She sighed impatiently.

"Of course I didn't know anything was going to happen – then," she said. "I mean, with the divining stick. I was just – practising. Then you came along and -" she bit her lip, "and I got mad, and it was completely weird - then the stick started twisting, I could hardly hold onto it, and the wall - just -"

She stopped talking and stared into his eyes, making him uneasy. There was a silence. He cast around for something to say.

"You were practising? Well, where did you get the stick from? How did you know what to do?"

Holly went on staring at him, and then to his complete surprise, she laughed.

"Well, that's just it," she said. "Oh God, and you think just that much is weird."

He was bemused.

"What? What Holly? What are you on about?"

She sat straighter.

"Ok," she said, and there was a steeliness in her voice. "Ok, Callum, I'm going to tell you – stuff. Just don't dare get smart – or think this is any kind of a laugh, or I swear I'll get you." She sounded serious.

He nodded, casually.

"And don't even think about telling Will. Or Duncan. Can you keep a secret?"

He nodded again.

Holly took a deep breath.

"I think it's all to do with Drum," she began. She started to describe her first meeting with Hawthorne Agnew.

"And there was a – sort of gypsy camp? On the other side of some old hurdles?" Callum could not keep the scepticism out of his voice. He told himself she must be expecting it.

He decided not to mention Doctor Sliddery and The Grete Herball yet. He was conscious of feeling relieved. The nutty stuff wasn't just him.

But no need to relieve Holly just yet.

Holly was flinching at his tone. "Well I don't know if Hawthorne's what you'd call a gypsy. There didn't seem to be anyone there but her. But she, sort of, knew Drum. I didn't really get it, but it was like Drum had been there before. She called him a galloway. And he likes her. He does just what she tells him."

Callum laughed out loud. "You've got to be kidding!"

Even Holly raised a faint smile.

"And then when I came back, I found I'd been away all day."

He stared at her.

"So you had." He considered. "That makes time travel a bit inconvenient. What if you find you've been gone months?"

"I know. Anyway, the next time, I took my lunch, and it seemed to be about right."

"Um."

He realised he believed her. Briefly he considered teasing her, but another look at her intense, fierce eyes deterred him. "And what happened that time?"

Holly explained about her walk into Wigtown, and Hawthorne's water divining job for the minister.

"And then Hawthorne gave me the divining stick. It's made of hazel. I was just looking up what the books say about it. She said," Holly's voice became very casual, "that I should practice, because I had a talent for it."

Callum raised his eyebrows, but said nothing. Actually, he could think of nothing you could say.

There was a short pause.

"The thing is," Holly said slowly, "Hawthorne never seems to be surprised by all this stuff. She said, to me and Drum, she said we'd been Travelling. Capital T. You could almost see it there, hanging in mid-air. I get the strong impression she was – almost expecting us?"

They both fell silent. Callum focussed on the flawed wavy glass of the sash window.

"Does that sound completely mad?" Holly said in a rather small voice.

Callum looked at her and grinned.

"Yup," he said. "Mind you, I mean that. It does. I don't understand a word of it."

She glared at him.

"But I believe you," he added hastily, "because of when the wall vanished, and that horse just trotted past. In another time zone," he added, in genuine wonderment.

"Hawthorne and Mr Wormelow's time zone," said Holly rather firmly.

"So when are we setting off?" said Callum. A trip through the wood with Drum and a decent picnic to visit a friendly gypsy woman beat a nasty ten minutes in the Gardening History Room with Doctor Sliddery any day.

Holly was suddenly looking much happier.

"Well, we can't today. It's already gone three. We probably wouldn't show up again till after midnight. Picture that."

Callum grinned. "Let's amaze my ma. We'll tell her we're both going on a picnic tomorrow. I'll take my bike. You're welcome to Drum."

# 14    The Darkment Knife

*On his table are bowls of bay, hellebore, lavender and rue. The bowls are grouped neatly among the glass retorts and alchemical vessels. She is trembling, gazing at a dusty spoon forgotten at the back, but without really seeing it.*

*The candle flickers in a draught.*

*He is sharpening his Darkment Knife on the fine whetstone, the thin sound rhythmic with his concentration.*

*Her thumping heart seems to echo the noise.*

*She wants to run, but the crow perched on the table's edge is watching her beadily.*

*He puts down the Knife, steps towards her and grasps her arm, holding her tightly just above the elbow.*

*"Stand still girl." He picks up a tiny silver dish with his other hand, positions it on the edge of the table.*

*"Never forget that you are atoning for your sin. Marked even as you are, I gave you shelter. Now you contribute to my advancement. I have given your miserable life purpose, when it had none before."*

*He is holding the Knife now.*

*Sparrow can hear a shallow gasping from somewhere close by, and dimly knows it as her own.*

*He positions her forearm above the silver dish, presses the gleaming blade against the skin of her inner elbow, then raises his hand to press the sharpened point through the* flesh. She whimpers, and her blood wells, and drips, into the silver dish.

"Hair" he says. She stands still, shaking, while the Darkment Knife cuts a hank of coarse dark hair from her head. Now she is allowed to clutch her wounded arm. Her blood stains her fingers.

He is busy now, with the curving glass retort suspended over a thin flame, conjuring his discovery. She knows now what he gains.

He cannot be young again, but he no longer ages.

"Get out girl."

Up in the cold attic, she lights a candle stub. She dresses the wound with a cobweb, then binds her arm with rags.

Afterwards, she sits on the edge of her lumpy mattress, holding her knees, winding her Red around, around and through her fingers, especially the last finger, the Mark, the one the Darkment chose.

She stops. And pulls forward her hair so the candlelight falls on it, and she can find the streak of white hair running through the black.

# 15 The Tinklers are Coming

Holly glanced over her shoulder, and for a moment watched Drum walking behind. Hawthorne held the end of his halter rope, and his muzzle bobbed, whiskery and obedient, by her hand as he carried the packs.

Callum walked beside her, wearing a shabby jacket and a worn pair of trousers that were too big for him. He looked younger, drowned in Hawthorne's eighteenth century cast-offs. Holly carried what was left of Liddy's picnic in a leather pouch on a cord across her shoulder. They had left Good Garden Books, and a puzzled, but undeniably well-pleased Liddy, straight after breakfast.

"Did you train him to have those on his back?" Holly asked Hawthorne. She waved at the weighty packs made from coarse hessian that were balanced across a small felt saddle on Drum's back. The ends of the packs hung low enough to bump on his forelegs. A dead rabbit dangled.

"Nay lass, but I need him to carry my spoons and wares to the Mercat, in Wigtown today. He just does, he just does."

Holly was most uncertain that Drum would just "do" back in the 21st century. But there he was a luxury and here he was a worker. She wondered if Callum noticed the difference in Drum's behaviour. He didn't seem all that interested in his mother's old pony a lot of the time. But he had been just as keen as her to take Drum to visit Hawthorne again, and to her relief they had easily found the gap by the hurdles into the wood. Now they were on one of Hawthorne's errands.

The little group plodded up the steep hill at Fountainblue. Holly noticed that the Victorian terraces weren't (as it were) there yet, and instead there were lower, simpler cottages, only one storey high, thatched instead of slated. She heard Callum's gasp as they reached the top and looked down North Main Street.

"This is very weird," he breathed.

Beyond the West Port, the cobbles of the Mercat Cross were covered by trestle tables, and milling knots of people. The tables were piled with goods and food, and Wigtown had clearly turned out in force to enjoy the Mercat. Holly looked further down to where the County Building should be. But it was obscured by a group of tall dark trees, which grew thickly in the middle of Main Street at its lower end.

"Where the bowling green is now," she thought to herself.

Hawthorne cast an appraising eye over Holly and Callum, as if measuring how well they blended in. She caught Holly's eye, and said softly, "Don't you talk".

So she watched as Hawthorne chatted easily to her acquaintances in the crowd, and when they had worked their way to the edge of Main Street she tethered Drum to a ring in the wall outside a butcher's window.

Hawthorne lifted down the dead rabbit from Drum's shoulders, put her head in through the door and called. A

88

heavy woman emerged, smiled at Hawthorne, accepted the rabbit and nodded at the tied-up pony. They had their pitch.

Holly and Callum helped Hawthorne unload Drum, and lay out the wares on a worn woollen rug on the wide pavement. Hawthorne seated herself on a high stone step conveniently near to her stock and sent Holly and Callum to squat under the wall of the shop beside where Drum was tethered.

Holly sat on her heels and felt Drum lip her hair. She hoped that was all he'd do. The pony sighed, tilted a hind hoof, and seemed to settle himself to wait. Callum, perched beside her on a tin box out of Drum's pack, leaned over.

"He's better behaved here", he whispered. "I mean now. Don't you think?"

"That's just it," said Holly eagerly, "I think it's not a coincidence. It's really strange. I think he knew who Hawthorne was, you know, that first time in the wood..."

She realised he had stopped listening to her. Her voice tailed away, and she followed his gaze.

A tall man had joined the back of the group that crowded around Hawthorne. The women laughed and cracked jokes as they bought and bartered.

But the man stood still.

Holly thought that even the man's face was still. He was dressed entirely in black, and wore a tall, brimmed hat, though most of the men were in shirtsleeves and bareheaded in the warm afternoon. Something about him made her feel uncomfortable. She noticed other people moved quietly out of his way.

He turned his head. Now he was staring at Callum.

Beside her, she sensed Callum freeze.

She sat taller, and stared at the man herself, to distract him. His gaze swung onto her face, and she felt the force of his eyes like a shock of cold water.

She gasped, and saw the man's thin mouth stretch slightly, humourlessly, and then suddenly he turned away, disturbing a group of crows which had been scavenging boldly on the cobbles among the market people. The birds cawed and flapped back into the darkness of the tall trees. Callum let out his breath.

"What?" said Holly. "Callum, who was –"
"Not now" he said, glowering.

Hawthorne walked across, her eyes on Callum's face. He looked up at her wordlessly. She looked steadily at him, and he dropped his eyes to avoid her.

Then "Look," she said, "The tinklers are coming."
And pointed.
Holly saw a lively, laughing group of people emerging from Lochan Croft. Striding at the front was a dark, lean,

energetic man, who even as they watched swung a fiddle to his shoulder and began to play. A squeezebox joined him, and a drum tucked under someone's arm. The exuberant music swelled to fill the marketplace as the tinklers approached, setting feet tapping. The musicians swung up North Main Street, followed by a noisy crowd, before turning away behind the tall trees.

The afternoon wore away slowly. Much to Holly and Callum's irritation, Hawthorne seemed not to want them to wander. They tried sidling off to inspect the other stalls, but she warned them back with a sharp look. "What did she bring us for?" Holly complained.

Callum shifted his feet suddenly. He glanced sideways at her.

"I think," he said warily, "maybe it was because of that man. You know, the tall, thin - freaky one, wearing black, the one – from this morning." He looked at Holly to check she understood him.

He hesitated, then seemed to make up his mind.

"I met him before. In the Gardening History Room at home. I think it's Doctor Sliddery. You know, the one who wrote No. 71's famous book."

He paused again. Then he explained about his misadventures with The Grete Herball.

When he had finished, Holly stared at him in hostile silence for a moment. She saw him shift uncomfortably.

"Yeah, well, you should have told me," she snapped. "Why didn't you tell me? Why didn't you tell me when I told you about Drum and Hawthorne?" She glared at him suspiciously.

Callum looked uneasy. "It never felt like the right time" he said lamely.

Holly stared at him. She shrugged coldly.

There was a very uncomfortable pause.

Then she said, "But didn't you ever look at that book before?"

"With my mum, I had. Nothing ever happened till this summer though."

"Are you hungered?" Hawthorne was bending over them. "Come with me now."

She led the way across to a stall on which stood a basket filled with warm pies. The fragrant smell drove out Holly's annoyance. Callum groaned with joy, earning himself a sharp look from Hawthorne. Holly held her tongue, and felt her stomach rumble.

"We'll take three, if you please," Hawthorne said to the stall-holder. Then she looked closer at the stallholder, and said, "Is that Margaret? It must be many a year!"

"It is indeed Margaret, Mistress Agnew, and 'deed it's been a verra long time." The woman behind the table put out a hand, and warmly laid it on the back of Hawthorne's own. "He got well again, you know, my boy. Taller than me, he is now, and working. I don't doubt I'd have lost him without your medicine. And then you never were back for me to thank you."

Hawthorne put down her packets and took the woman's hand between both of hers. "Then I'm right glad to stand here now and hear that news."

The woman beamed and gathered up three pies. She piled them up and put them in Holly's slightly startled hands. The pies were warm and fragrant. "This'll be your lassie now, Mistress Agnew? My, but she's grown into a tall bonny one."

Holly was embarrassed, but through her confusion she saw Hawthorne's face close. It was suddenly full of sadness.

"Nay, mistress, I'm minding these bairns for my cousin today. I lost my ain wee one these seven years gone."

The woman's face grew sad too. She put her hand out and touched Hawthorne's arm again.

Holly passed the pies round and they moved away. Mouths full, they followed her across the cobbles to join a crowd gathering around the tinkler musicians, who had reappeared and seemed to be setting up by the Mercat Cross.

Holly glanced up at Hawthorne's face as they edged their way in, looking for that sadness she'd just seen at the pie stall. But Hawthorne's brown face was calm again. She looked down at Holly and smiled very gently.

The music was fast now, inviting the first dancers, who were getting up and swinging each other round. Hawthorne found a space and sat herself down between a loudly

93

clapping family and a bony old man who just sucked on a clay pipe and nodded, eyes shut. Holly and Callum squeezed in next to Hawthorne, and squatted down. A fold of Hawthorne's voluminous skirt draped over the hem of Holly's authentically threadbare borrowed one.

The skies were paling over the rooftops, and now the music was like a rich slumberous spell, carrying Holly away.

She was fascinated by the fiddler. The tune would be carried by the squeezebox player and the drummer, and then the fiddler would give the crowd a glinting grin and swing his wide shoulders with a swagger, as he twisted the fiddle under his chin and loosed the tune, sending it soaring high above the broad, slow melody.

The great, drowsy music flowed in its rhythms over the listeners, drawing each of them in to themselves, following their paths through memory and feeling.

Then Holly saw the fiddler square up, and the swing of his broad shoulders as the fiddle forged again ahead of the tune, lifting it with a piercing, intense sweetness that made the little hairs stand up along her arms and at the back of her head.

She felt herself bond with the crowd, believing together for a few moments in all that was good in the world. The tender fiddle lifted them slowly, cushioned them all against fear and pain, although all the fear and pain of the world was mourned in the breaking notes. And then the rhythm from the squeezebox and the drum carried them on again until the fiddle caught up the first slow notes of the sweeter, keener tune, rearing higher and higher, full of joy.

Holly sat below the Mercat Cross, and loved everyone. She thought of Stan, and with a surge of generosity, of Liddy. She was amazed by the variety and beauty of her existence and then, all too soon, it was over.

There was a moment's pause. Then a soft sigh rose from the crowd squatting on the cobbles in the dusk of this different century. And then they called out and burst into clapping. Holly looked around and saw Hawthorne beside her wiping away a tear. Another one trickled slowly, unnoticed, down her brown cheek, lodging for a moment in a deepening wrinkle near her mouth.

"Och, he can play like an angel and like a devil, can Lev," she said.


Lev.

Holly was looking back at the fiddler, thinking how handsome he was (though he was quite old, he might be thirty), when he caught her eye and smiled. She felt as if a spotlight had been turned on her.

His smile was kind, but contained a teasing awareness of his own dark attractiveness that plunged her into confusion. She wrenched her eyes away, stared at her feet and was appalled to her bones to know that Hawthorne, who missed nothing, must have noticed.


But in the pause Hawthorne was leaning behind Holly to speak to Callum. "Dinnae fret", she was saying softly, "our Wigtown's Doctor Sliddery won't never stay when there's

95

music. Aye Callum, I saw him too.  This is his time as it's mine. He'd suspect. But he'd not know you, would he?"

Holly saw Callum relax, just a little.

"He could hear me, but not see me, before, you know, in our time," he whispered to Hawthorne.

Then, "But how did you know?"


Hawthorne smiled but did not respond and Holly glared at Callum, irritated at all the secrecy, feeling excluded. She stared hard at the side of his face, willing him to look up, but he didn't.


The music re-started and the dancing began in earnest. Whirling skirts and an alarming combination of bare feet and laced up clogs swung and stamped inches away from Hawthorne and the children. It was impossible not to smile, not to laugh, with the dancers.

Heavy middle-aged women swung by on their partner's sinewy forearms. A toothless man, bent by labour, laughed raucously as he spun his partner, young enough to be a daughter.  She whirled away from him, for a moment dancing alone, her glimmering raven hair streaming behind her where it was coming down from its bun. Her face was bold and radiant, and Holly saw her vivid dark gaze lock for a moment with the fiddler's, and saw how his eyes followed her.

Sometime later, in a pause in the music and dancing, Hawthorne urged Holly and Callum to their feet, yawning and stretching stiff legs.

They packed up Hawthorne's stall and loaded Drum, who by now was no longer very co-operative, even for Hawthorne. Slowly they left the music and the singing behind as they plodded wearily down out of Wigtown. The evening was cooling, and darkness not far away.

"Who was the black-haired girl dancing?" Holly asked. She could not ask about the fiddler.

"Yon bonny one? That would be the Ursari girl. A tinkler family, to you. They call her Ana. She came here with her family from Hungary, or Romania or some such. There's a deal of trouble around that lassie."

"What do you mean Hawthorne?"

"Well, she turns heads. And some say she's a wild one. *I* like her" said Hawthorne decidedly, "Some folks are just jealous, I reckon. And Ana, she has her own mind, and it's not the same as her father's. He'd marry her off to his own choosing. And that's not the same as Ana's choosing."

When they reached Hawthorne's clearing, Callum said, "I wish we could just sleep here", but Hawthorne looked horrified, and packed them back off through the hurdles. She only let them pause for long enough to make them change their clothes.

"When will we see you again?" Holly asked her.

A thin twig swung gently in a breath of wind and prodded her as she felt her way towards the hurdles in the almost-dark of Hawthorne's wood, following the deeply reluctant Drum, who was being towed along by Callum.

"You'll see me when you do. Keep this by you when you travel." Holly felt Hawthorne press a leafy sprig of something into her hand.

"What -?"

"Tis thyme. It helps."

Then Holly found she was stumbling through the hurdles, and already the ground beneath her feet was the stubble after the baler had been over, and they were back, and she was relieved to see it was still daylight in the 21st century.

# 16   I want to speak
## to the bear tamers

*Eyes downcast, she hurries along the pavement of North Main Street, towards the West Port, with the stiff envelope for Mr Wormelow clutched in her hand. She does not look at anyone she passes on the road, nor does she speak. All the same, she knows when they recoil on seeing her. She thrusts her left hand deeper into her shawl.*

*At the gates of the new manse, she hesitates. Then she steps carefully around the builders' litter to reach the grand new front door. Again, she hesitates.*

*Then raises her hand and pulls the bell. When the door opens there is a neat maid in a black dress trimmed with lace, a starched white apron drawn on over the top. At the sight of Sparrow she stiffens, then takes the outstretched envelope with exaggerated care, without touching fingers. She bobs once, then shuts the door smartly.*

*Sparrow picks her way back to the manse gates. She pauses on the road, then seemingly makes up her* mind and  sets off determinedly towards the Inks, down by the harbour.

Even from some distance away, she can smell the wood smoke and see the benders.  They seem to clutch downwards, clinging  to the cold earth in the chilly spring wind blowing in across the Irish Sea.  She feels panic rise in her chest, and crushes it back.

She approaches an old woman crouched over a fire.

"I want to speak to the bear tamers."

She hears her own voice sound so thin, so easy to ignore.

But the old woman nods, turns and calls out to a bender further back, half hidden by a clump of gorse bushes.

A dark young woman emerges, head bent, and then she straightens gracefully.  She picks up two pails of water, and walks steadily towards Sparrow.

"I am Ana.  I am of the Ursari.  Who wants to know?"

They speak together, low-voiced, heads bent, their backs turned to the cold breeze.  Sparrow's voice is very low.

"Doctor Sliddery!  You work in his house!" Ana's eyes flash, and Sparrow shrinks.  "Wait, I have to tell you - I tell you about my aunt, and then you must leave, you must run away."

Sparrow murmurs again, and Ana replies.

"No, the Ursari did not lose you. Some other mother searches for you, I think. Twenty summers ago, we lost my aunt. She was young, she worked with the bears with her sister, my mother. She was Ursari, she was one of us. And we lost her. He stole her, he used her up to make him young."

Ana draws herself up proudly, and a black curl, shiny as coal, escapes from the scarf holding her hair. "Child, you must run away. We, the Ursari, have come here to make an end with Dr. Sliddery."

Ana takes Sparrow by the hand and leads her round the gorse bushes. In a pen made of stakes and brushwood, a brown bear rears up suddenly onto his hind legs, sniffing the air. Sparrow freezes.

Ana strokes her hair, and slowly, Sparrow becomes calm.

# 17    A Notable Herbalist

Rain battered on the glass roof of the conservatory, then sluiced downwards in endless rivulets.  No. 71 seemed dark and chilly in the change of weather.  Holly, mooching around after breakfast, slumped listlessly onto a conservatory chair.  She watched Liddy's runner beans soak up the downpour outside.

"You'd never catch Drum in this anyway."  Callum came in and flopped onto a chair opposite her.  "He doesn't do working in bad weather."

"I expect he would if Hawthorne told him to" said Holly, but she grinned.

"Yes.  'Spect he would" said Callum.  "We don't know why though, do we?  I mean, we don't know much about Hawthorne."

"What are you getting at?"  Holly was instantly suspicious.

Callum put up his hands.  "Chill, Holly, I just said we don't actually know much about her.  And, er, we don't."

Holly said nothing.

Callum continued, "It just does occur to me, she knows about Doctor Sliddery, even seems to know I met him.  How come we met her?  Why did she take us to the market?  So he could see us?"

"Callum, I just know Hawthorne's alright!" Holly stood up. "I've met her twice more than you have! She knows about all sorts of stuff – I dunno why, or how. But she's good! She's kind. And Drum trusts her."

"So he's a good judge of character! Get real Holly!" Callum snorted. "Does it not strike you Hawthorne's got all the characteristics of a witch?" He took in Holly's expression. "Ok, Ok, maybe a white witch – but, definitely, a bit witchy?"

"Who's witchy?" Liddy came through the door from the kitchen. "No, don't answer that Callum. It might be better to pretend I didn't hear you. I need your help, folks."

"I'll help." Holly got up quickly.

"Well, both of you really. There's a guy, an archivist from Edinburgh University, he's coming to visit me this morning, in, erm -" she twisted her watch over on her wrist so she could see it – "in about five minutes actually. Unless he's late."

She looked at them hopefully.

"You want us to mind the shop?" said Holly.

"And keep half an eye on the café too – just till Alison gets in? Hence both of you. I'll reward you – somehow."

"We will be richly rewarded with rich riches, one day" said Callum solemnly.


They followed her out of the conservatory towards the shop.

"What's he want ma?" Callum seemed curious.

"He's very excited about The Grete Herball. You know I gave it a mention on No. 71's blog – it's just a good story, Holly. How I came here, filled with ambition to run a gardening bookshop in Scotland's book town, a single parent with no time, not enough money, but a dab hand at putting up shelves? And how I grubbed around in the cellar and found Doctor Sliddery's Grete Herball wrapped up in a deerskin inside an old wooden box? It was right at the back, under a pile of mouldy World War I greatcoats and a dead rat. Yuck." Liddy checked the cash register rapidly, slammed the cash drawer shut and turned the key.

"But that must have been fantastic!" Holly stared into space, imagining it. "Well, not the rat. But isn't the book really valuable?"

"We do hope so." Callum rubbed his nose meaningfully with one finger.

"Well, so-so," said Liddy, more cautiously. "Then again, it might well be more valuable just as the curiosity that makes Good Garden Books special. Whatever, it's good he wants to come and see it. Mr Drouth, I think he said." She disappeared rapidly into the Gardening History Room, her red plait swinging vigorously.

"Well." Holly sat down on the chair by the till. "You can do the café Callum."

"Oh waily, waily, waily." Callum wandered back through the archway at the end of the hall and vanished into the café.

Holly rummaged under the table with the cash register on it, and found an old Beano annual. It was still early, still raining, and the shop was quiet. She was nostalgically enjoying the Bash Street Kids when the inner door opened.

Holly looked up.

A neat, slightly plump man stood dripping on the doormat. He wore a light brown tweed suit, and a mustard bow tie. In one hand he carried an antique leather Gladstone bag. With his other hand he shook raindrops off a flat tweed cap. He inspected the cap, looked up and saw Holly.

"Good morning young lady." He had a small, pale, pointy beard, but no moustache. "Mr Crispin Drouth." He held out a small, plump, pale hand.

"Hi" said Holly, unwillingly extending her own, and deeply grateful for Liddy's arrival at that moment from the doorway of the Gardening History Room. Mr Drouth turned his back instantly on Holly, and strode towards Liddy, hand still outstretched. "Mr Crispin Drouth" he repeated. "Delighted, really delighted."

Liddy swept him away into the Gardening History Room, hissing "Coffee?" imploringly at Holly as she went. Holly put up a thumb, then rolled her eyes and headed for the café.

"He sounds every bit as weird as you'd expect." Callum passed down two mugs to Holly. "Wonder what he knows about nasty Doctor Sliddery though. Even weirder that we can't tell him. Shall we eavesdrop?"

They loaded a clean tray with mugs, cafetiere and milk, pinched two flapjacks from the display unit and put them on a plate. Then Holly led the way back to the Gardening History Room. The door was pushed to, but not shut. They eavesdropped.

"- fascinating, of course, because this is perhaps the only surviving copy. You didn't realise? Well, of course highly controversial, in its day, yes, but nowadays still – a rather – ha – *hot* potato!"

Holly and Callum hesitated. Holly propped the edge of the tray on the edge of the dado rail to help hold its weight.

"Truly, I had no idea" Liddy was saying. "Never really had time to look very far into it, except I had the impression that he was really very obscure, virtually forgotten. I supposed he was only of interest in Wigtownshire."

"Actually a *little* bit of a scandal." Mr Drouth's voice rose archly. "Suppressed by the Victorians, and the Church. I think they thought he'd gone a bit *far*."

"What the –" muttered Callum, and kicked open the door.

"No!" Holly hissed at him, then as the door swung wider, she stepped forward, beamed at Liddy and Mr Drouth and said hospitably, "Coffee."

106

"You nit" she said to Callum, back in the café. "We were about to learn something."

"Oh alright then."

They returned to the hallway, and loitered, ears flapping.

"- never took that chapter very seriously – no, really, I'm sure he was just a bit of a charlatan -"

"Actually, I can assure you, Ms Murray, that Doctor Sliddery believed that the chapter in question did record a matter of reality. Some even said there had been – ah - *experiments*."

"Ugh, how horrible! All the same, you must agree the language of the day was often figurative – all his stuff about gleaning years – see, here it is – I'm sure he was just being metaphorical. And other sources place him as a respected member of the community, friend of the minister, what was he called – funny name – Wormelow?"

"Yes, that's right." Mr Drouth's voice filled with admiration. "And there is no doubt Sliddery was a *notable* herbalist, indeed a scientist, in his way. He called himself 'hermetic doctor', and I rather think he liked to think of himself as an alchemist. And of course, he was a competent artist – he did all his own woodcuts for the Herball. Nonetheless, I must admit to being very interested in his – ah – *darker* chapters. Indeed, I came here to day very much hoping to gain permission to study the manuscript."

107

Outside the door, Callum and Holly exchanged looks.

Liddy prevaricated. "Mr Drouth, I really can't let the manuscript go up to Edinburgh."

"Ms Murray, I wouldn't dream of requesting that it did! No, no, my suggestion is merely to study the book here, in the security of your own bookshop! Only for a day or two, I can put up in a bed and breakfast. I promise I'll be fully out of your way, Ms Murray, before the Book Festival!"

The shop door opened suddenly, letting in a sudden coolness and the sound of spray from the street as a very wet family of five entered Good Garden Books. "Oh thank God, I can smell coffee!" exclaimed a harassed parent. Three small dripping children escaped into the bookshop.

Holly motioned to Callum, welcomed the customers and led the way through to the café.

The coffee shop proved unexpectedly popular over the next two hours, and even when Alison arrived to cook lunches, Callum and Holly were kept busy taking orders, serving and clearing tables. Holly enjoyed chatting to the customers. Callum got by with nodding at them. Liddy emerged after an hour, grimaced at Holly and reassured a couple dithering in the doorway of the Gardening History Room:

"No, no, it's fine, do go on in. Mr Drouth is from Edinburgh University, here to do some research on The Grete Herball. He has just assured me you won't distract him!" She beamed at the couple, and then made for the café and the teapot.

"Is he still here?" Callum was incredulous. "It's nearly dinner time."

Liddy sighed, poring over book orders. "I took him another cup of tea an hour ago. He seems completely gripped. He's already arranged to be back here at nine tomorrow. That's if we can ever persuade him to leave for his B&B tonight."

"Does he know much about Doctor Sliddery already?" Holly asked carefully.

"Dunno. I suppose he must. He just said Doctor Sliddery was a wise man and a healer." Liddy lifted a pile of paper, searched underneath it, then sighed. She leaned down to peer under the table. "I've lost a bill."

"No worries then" said Callum cheerfully.

Liddy emerged from under the table with the missing bill in her hand. "However he also seems to think Doctor Sliddery was rather a controversial character too. Actually, there's a couple of chapters in the Grete Herball which I've always thought were, well, a bit unpleasant. Mr Drouth seems fascinated with them."

"How unpleasant?  How d'you mean?" Callum clearly thought he was onto something.  Holly scowled at him warningly.

"Oh, just full of his obsession to live forever.  He was full of crazy schemes for cheating death and ageing.  He'd probably be into cryogenics if he was alive now.  He had a particularly nasty idea about "gleaning" years from people who were still very young.  Well it sounds nasty because he's so mysterious about it.  He never quite says what he means, but you're left thinking he probably had his drawbacks as a member of the human race.  Mr Drouth thinks he was a genius though, far as I can make out."

Liddy rose from her desk.

"Time to make dinner.  Be about an hour."  She disappeared through the door marked "Private".

"Did you hear that?" Callum rounded on Holly.  "I'm not at all sure about that guy Drouth.  Goes without saying I'm no fan of Doctor S either.  'Had his drawbacks as a member of the human race'!  What an understatement!"

Holly nodded absently.  Then she looked up.  "Isn't it a bit fishy that Mr Drouth should turn up now?  I mean, with all this going on?  If we can step between times, who is he?  And whose side is he on?"

"Good point."  He considered.  "Perhaps we should tail him when he leaves here tonight?  We might find out something, at least."

"Yeah, we'd know which B&B he's staying at" said Holly sarcastically. But she agreed to the tailing idea, mostly because she didn't like Mr Drouth's pointy beard.

They sloped off to hang around in the Square.

# 18    Look Well Before

"Hope he's not going to be much longer" said Callum. He was getting hungry. "It must be nearly dinner time. At least it's stopped raining." He stuck his head out from the doorway where they were waiting, and peered down the street. "In fact it's quite nice now."

"Shut up, this is him" Holly hissed.

They watched Mr Drouth step neatly down from the front door of Good Garden Books and Callum distinctly heard Liddy bolt it behind him. He hoped she was hurrying back to the kitchen to produce food.

Mr Drouth adjusted his tweed cap fussily in the warm evening sunlight and set off at a brisk pace in the direction of the County Building. Callum nudged Holly, and they wandered casually after him. He was easy to spot among the groups of tourists and early evening dog walkers. He paused by the door of the County Building and read a notice board, then turned the corner and set off down Harbour Road.

"Come on!" Callum broke into a run, and then they both skidded to a halt by the corner of Harbour Road. They peered round, and were just in time to see Mr Drouth step into the doorway of a neat Bed and Breakfast embellished with red geraniums in hanging baskets.

"Oh." Callum was disappointed.

"Well he might come out again. It could be a false lead," said Holly. "Perhaps we'd better wait."

"A stake-out," said Callum sarcastically. They stood indecisively by the County Building's railings. Behind them, someone shouted something and a car's tyres squealed. It hooted its horn.

"Now what?" Holly turned, then grabbed Callum's arm. "Callum - it's Drum – be quick - "

She began to run, and Callum, seeing the situation that was unfolding at the other side of the County Building, ran too.


Drum was out in the road, no longer a quiet old pony. Traffic had stopped and people on pavements were panicking and shouting for their young children. Drum, wild eyed, shied away from the front of a camper van and broke into a canter, his hooves clattering noisily on tarmac, tail up, mane flying. He flung up his head at a man who snatched at him and plunged round the corner at a panicky canter, towards Holly and Callum.

"Whoa, now, Drum, whoa boy!" Holly planted herself in the pony's path, and he braked, front hooves skidding slightly on tarmac, legs braced.

"Now then, Drum" said Callum, intensely relieved. "Grab him quick, Holly."

Holly was already slipping her arms round Drum's neck. "Good boy, you're OK now. Give me your hoodie Callum, it'll do to hold him."

Callum squirmed out of it, trying not to alarm the pony with waving arms. He passed it to Holly who slid it round Drum's neck where her arms had been. Drum sighed suddenly, lowered his head and blew out through his nose.

"Who the heck rattled your cage?" said Callum, patting Drum's sweaty neck. "How did you get out anyway?"

"Has he done it before?" asked Holly, starting to turn the pony round in the road. "It's alright" she called to a man hurrying towards them, "he's ours. I don't know how he got out, but we'll sort it out, thanks." The man waved and disappeared back into the County Buildings.

"You mean has he got out before? Well not like this. Not appeared on North Main Street like Champion the Wonder Horse," said Callum. He was into retro TV.

"Usually if he gets out he's on the nearest grass verge, stuffing his face."

Drum plodded beside Holly, looking harmless.

Reassuring various neighbours and helpful tourists they made their way back down North Main Street in the direction of Drum's field. Drum, who seemed to be hungry after all the excitement, realized that with only a sweatshirt wrapped round his neck, he was effectively free to graze. He dragged Holly across the pavement and took a large bite out of a tub of petunias.

"No! No! Drum, head up!" Holly hauled at the pony without effect. "Help me Callum!"

Callum heaved with all his strength, and together they dragged him out of the flowers and shoved him forwards for a few exhausting steps before he was snatching at smartly mown grass by a garden gate.

"This is hopeless," Callum said. "Look, you stay with him, I'll run home and get the halter. And tell Liddy. Good luck – he likes flowers."

"Smart move Callum."

By the time Callum came running back, halter dangling from his hand, Holly was busy apologizing to the owner of the petunias, who had most unluckily come out of his front door and noticed the gap. They got the halter on Drum, Callum reclaimed his hoodie, and Holly yanked the pony's head up and they set off again.

"Ma says will we try to see how he got out and fix it just for now, I've got binder twine in my pocket. And she says she's leaving our dinner in the warming oven, she's got a booksellers' meeting tonight."

What Liddy had actually said was, "What a mercy Holly was there. Tell her thank you very much." Callum felt that this could wait.

At the church gate Drum stopped. Holly tugged on the halter. The pony let her stretch out his neck, but he wouldn't move his hairy feet.

"Bloody animal! Why do we keep him?" Callum leaned on Drum's hindquarters, desisting smartly when the pony laid back his ears and raised his hind leg threateningly.

115

"What's up Drum?" Holly was more patient. "Come on boy, don't you want to get back to your own grass?" She tried to make him step sideways, but the pony took her by surprise and forged ahead right through the church gates.

"Help, where's he going now?" Holly hauled on the rope, but Drum dragged her onto the grass between the old gravestones.

"God, we're in trouble now!" said Callum. He grabbed the rope too, and felt old gravestones under his feet as Drum hauled them forward. He got the giggles. "Hey - Holly, did you hear what I said – we're in trouble with God!"

"Callum, shut up!" gasped Holly, "and help me!"

Drum took another step, and neatly nipped the heads off some roses in a jar wedged into the corner of a grave surround.

Callum heaved alongside Holly, and they managed to haul up his head and turn him round. He immediately plunged his nose back into the grass.

"Holly. Look at that." Callum let go of Drum and pointed.

A few steps in front of where Drum was now enthusiastically tearing grass, was an old headstone. It leaned slightly, and was green and mossy with age. Holly slackened her grasp on the halter rope.

The inscription on the stone was worn, and partially obscured by lichen. With difficulty they read:

JARED SLIDDERY,

116

HERMETIC DOCTOR

OF WIGTOWNE.

BORN 21 DECEMBER 1691


LOOK WELL BEFORE

TAKE HEED BEHIND.

BEWARE BY ME

MIND WELL THE END.


Under the inscription were carved a skull ("Unpleasantly detailed" said Callum), and an hourglass.

"Just a minute" said Holly, concentrating. "Callum, look, look when it says he was born – he can't have been, because -"

"Because what?"

"Because," Holly frowned, "when I asked Hawthorne, she said it was "the year of Mister Wormelow's Lord, 1797.""

"So?" Callum wasn't really listening. A snowflake had just fluttered down and landed on the back of his hand.

Another one landed on his cheek. He shivered. It was getting colder every minute. Snowflakes began to star the green top of the gravestone. Then more fell, and more. And suddenly, the air was filled with snow.

Callum stared wildly round. The warm summer evening was gone as if it never had been. Drum stood alert, with his head up, ears pricked. Darkness was falling.

"Holly" said Callum. He kept his voice very quiet. "Something's up."

"I know." She sounded serious. "Wow, just look at this snow."

The snow was already several centimetres deep. It stuck to the gravestones, lay like a thin blanket on Drum's back.

"I'm glad I went back for the halter" said Callum.

"You what?" said Holly, not taking her eyes off the snowy graveyard.

"It meant I got my hoodie back."

"Well I'm wearing mine too, and I'm still freezing." Holly looked suddenly decisive. "I think we should shelter till we can work out what's going on."

She pulled at the halter and turned Drum round.

"Er, Holly. Look. Doctor Sliddery's gravestone's gone" said Callum, pointing. She stopped, and they both stared at the smooth, unbroken snow where the headstone had been only moments before.

"In fact, this graveyard's nothing like so well populated as it was." He saw Holly step forward, tugging at Drum's halter. "Where are you going Holly?"

"The church porch. At least we can shelter for a minute." She looked back at him for a moment. "Well yes. You're right about the graveyard. I don't think this is the 21st century any more, Callum. Not so many dead people."

"That's one way to put it," said Callum, following her.

118

The snow whirled dizzying patterns in the dim, flickering lamplight that was coming from a quaint old lantern on the church gate. Holly began to walk towards the church. She warmed her cold fingers under Drum's mane. The pony came obediently now, following Holly up the path, his hooves muffled by snow. Callum's trainers crunched in the snow behind them. Otherwise, it was very quiet. The church porch was just visible, behind a tracery of black boughs which swayed against the dimming sky.

"Wait. There's someone there," Callum said quietly. Holly tightened her grip on the rope, and Drum stopped. They listened.

From the church porch, a man's voice was singing, very softly. Holly and Callum and the pony stood still, half hidden behind a great black yew tree at the side of the path. Then Holly saw someone else come lightly around the corner of the church, a slim, upright figure swathed in shawls, long skirts rustling. Holly caught a glimpse of a young, eager face, and a mass of tumbling dark curls.

"Ana" she whispered to Callum. He nodded, and the singer stepped out of the dark porch, silent now, his arms outstretched. Ana ran straight into them.

"Oh cringe!" whispered Callum.

He buried his face in Drum's mane. Holly saw Lev, for it was certainly Lev the fiddle player, bend his face to Ana's. She didn't want to watch – but she did.

She wondered how she and Callum could get away without being seen.

119

Drum, bored, stepped suddenly out round the yew tree. He dragged Holly and Callum with him again, and Ana let out a short, quickly stifled, cry of surprise.

"I remember you" said Lev, looking at Holly. She felt herself blushing, and was grateful it was dark. They were all squeezed into the church porch, sitting on one of the stone benches that ran down either side. Drum stood with his head drooping, sleeping on his feet now, in front of the other bench. Melting snow dripped from his back and legs onto the tiled floor.

"I do not," said Ana. "Who are you? Something is not right."

Callum smiled at her.

"Ana, this is Holly Berry, and I am Callum Murray. We come from the future" he added with obvious enjoyment.

Ana looked into his face. His grin faded as her examination of him continued. "But why are you here?" she asked. Her accent was strong and foreign, but she had no difficulty in believing them, Holly noticed.

"We don't really know why" she answered carefully. "It just keeps happening. It's something to do with him" she indicated the sleeping pony, "and Hawthorne Agnew. And Doctor Sliddery."

Ana's eyes widened for a moment. She took Lev's hand.

"I meet a child," she said slowly. "She is servant of Doctor Sliddery. She is afraid." Ana's vast dark eyes surveyed Holly and Callum slowly. "Maybe that is why you are here."

120

Callum gave her a straight look. "What do you know about Doctor Sliddery?" he asked.

Ana's eyes narrowed suddenly. "He is very bad. A wicked man. Perhaps you have come to help us, help the Ursari."

"I'm sorry Ana," said Holly, "Who are the Ursari?"

Lev leaned forwards. "They are the bear tamers." he said softly. "Come with us."

He stood, and, with some difficulty, because of Drum, who now did not want to move, everyone followed him back out of the porch.


It was still snowing, but less thickly than before. Lev led the way round the back of the church, one arm around Ana. Holly noticed that Ana, who moved like a dancer, didn't look as if she needed any support to walk through the snow.

Drum dug in his heels abruptly, jerking up his head. He blew urgently out through his nostrils.

"Oh come *on* Drum!" Holly was exasperated with him. Then she saw his eyes, very awake now, shining with fear. His front legs scrabbled at the snow in his urgency to back away.


Ana walked forward, as Lev put out his hand to keep Holly and Callum back. Then he put the hand next to Holly's on the halter rope and took a firm grip on Drum, who snorted, shuffled sideways, and stood uneasily still.

Ana called, a long, strange call, and waited, standing still in the snow, her shadow faint and long from the lantern light on the gate.

From a thicket of snow-covered brambles under the graveyard wall something was pushing its way out.

Holly could just make out a burly shape on all fours. There was something shaggy, and powerful in the way it buffeted the thick, arching brambles aside.

Drum let out a snort of fear, and Lev took tighter hold of him as the creature swung effortlessly onto its hind legs, rearing up to inspect them all.

It was a brown bear.

Chaos broke out on Church Lane. All at once, Holly saw men running, shouting, pulling open the back gate into the churchyard. Bare flames flared from torches.

"I'll not have you tinklers despoil our kirk!" roared a deep voice.

"You two!" Lev gripped the alarmed Drum with one hand and caught hold of Holly with the other. "Time you were away – get yourselves gone out of the churchyard by the front gate. Get on him – he'll go alright now he's seen what he's seen!"

He flung Holly up onto Drum's snowy back, flicked the halter rope up into her hand, and legged Callum up behind her.

"Go!" he said again, and clapped Drum hard on the hindquarters. The pony took off through the snow with a wild bound, Holly and Callum clinging on desperately. Behind them they heard men's raised voices, a dreadful growling snarl, and Ana shrieked angrily.

Then Holly and Callum had no time to do anything but hold on, as Drum lunged across the white graveyard, somehow missing the headstones in his panicky dash. With a grunt he scrambled down a steep bank and landed on the broader path to the main gate. It was snow covered, but level, and for once Drum had, as Callum commented later, the right idea. He fled out through the gates and turned sharp left downhill in the direction of his field.

"Holly" gasped Callum, clinging and jolting behind her, "Holly, the snow's gone!"

Drum steadied back into a trot, and then walked, and then stopped. He was breathing heavily.

Holly could smell honeysuckle, wafting from the hedge on warm evening air.

Callum slid down, and Holly followed him. Drum's field gate was just across the lane. Their fingers tingled painfully as they began to warm up.

# 19    Unusually Old

"See here, Callum, there's something really weird going on." Holly had been giving careful thought to the events of the night before. She looked earnestly at him.

"You don't say."

She was getting used to him. "Didn't you notice Doctor Sliddery's gravestone?  I tried to say, but then it started snowing."

Callum's Fab dripped on his knee and she watched him begin to lick the bottom of it carefully.  They were sitting on a bench in the gardens in the middle of town. Behind them came the faint click of balls on the bowling green.  It was very hot for south west Scotland.  Callum seemed to be trying to look intelligent, peering up at her sideways as he rescued his ice lolly.

"I mean," she persisted, "didn't you notice it had no date of death on it?  I thought they always did."

"True.  Very strange.  I noticed it had a truly spooky verse on it" Callum said.  "Look Well Before, something, something, something, Beware by Me, Mind Well The End – I'd go back and have another look except the weather's nice today.  It was a bit nippy round old Sliddery's gravestone last night.  Except of course, as we noticed, the snow made it do a vanishing act."

"But," said Holly, "Didn't you notice his date of birth? 1691? I thought The Grete Herball was still being written in 1797? And you told me it was published in 1809."

Callum stared seriously at his Fab, then looked up again at Holly. "That does make him unusually old, even for an author" he said carefully.

He met Holly's fierce expression, and added "Sorry – that is really weird. I mean really. He should be dead by then, especially in the eighteenth century."

"Especially in the eighteenth century? Were people more especially dead then?"

"Oh" she added, "you mean people didn't live so long."

"Maybe we made a mistake. Or the stonecarver did, on the gravestone. If he was anything like that old, he'd be famous. Like that tinkler – the King of the Galloway Gypsies, who was supposed to have died at 128 or something..."

"Great idea!" said Holly, slinging her own lolly stick in the bin by the seat. "Get up, now – we're going back to ask Liddy if Doctor Sliddery was famous."

In the sudden blissful cool of the hall of No. 71 they found Liddy gathering shopping bags. She held a shopping list in one hand and a pencil between her teeth.

"There you are" she said, removing it for a moment, "I'm just on my way to Newton Stewart. Do you want to come? Alison's in, so the shop's OK."

"S' too hot mum," Callum draped himself limply against the banisters.

125

"Actually" said Holly nonchalantly, "I just felt like staying in the shop and reading. I thought I'd just look, you know, through the glass, at your special book. The one by Doctor Sliddery?"

Liddy picked up her bags. "That's fine, I'm not expecting Mr Drouth till later." she hunted for her car keys, glanced up and grinned at them, "And as it's you, the key to the case is in the drawer. Just don't spill anything on the good Doctor!"

She headed for the doorway. Holly sprang after her.

"Thank you! We won't! Er, Liddy – was he famous, Doctor Sliddery? I mean, did everyone know about him here?"

Liddy slung the bags into her battered car and turned round.

"Well of course I think he's pretty important! He lived here, and he wrote that book. Mind you, when I went to the local archives find out more, they hadn't got any records of him. Told me they thought the mice must have been at them."

She went round to the other side of the car and got in, winding down windows urgently.

"Phew, it's like an oven in here! – have you been down to the churchyard yet Holly? He's got a very odd gravestone – his birth date would make him well over a hundred when he wrote The Grete Herball - I've always thought the stonemason must have been having an off day!"

She drove off, waving.

126

"What are people like?" said Callum as they retreated back into the cool of the bookshop. "You face them with the evidence, and they just laugh about it."

"Be fair," said Holly, "no-one's faced Liddy with Hawthorne Agnew and Doctor Sliddery."

They went to see Alison, who was reading peacefully in the café, waiting for customers to come back from the coast as the afternoon cooled.

"No bother" she said comfortably to them. "You go ahead and look at it, we won't get busy till later."

In the Gardening History Room the air was very still and cool. They shut the door. Holly walked over to the pale marble fireplace and leaned her hot cheek against it. Callum was fishing the key out of the drawer.

"I've never actually been allowed to do this, you know" he said. "And typically, now I am I'm not that sure I want to. When we look at this, suppose we end up with Doctor S again."

"Well, it would be interesting for me." Holly left the fireplace and leaned in over the book. "Anyway, didn't you say he couldn't even see you?"

"He could hear me though! And honestly, Holly, it's not a bit like meeting Hawthorne."

He unlocked the case.

Holly reached out a finger and gently traced the leather tooling on the cover. She opened the book and breathed in its smell.

"It's weird, just knowing he handled these pages. I rather like the woodcuts."

The heavily inked black and white illustrations coiled and blocked their way across the pages. A curving snake twisted its blunt nose and forked tongue to make a capital S. Sinister leaves grew rampantly up a margin. A creature with a bird's head, but a dragon's body twisted its head back and gripped its tail between its teeth, its eye blank, reptilian. Black flower heads nodded over gleaming knives.

"It's just after this, I remember it," Callum pointed to a fish which tipped a broad goblet to its lips with long fins.

"Sorry, what is?"

"The page where he is" Callum laid his hand onto the pages, to stop her turning them over.

"Callum, will you stop it!" Holly was getting annoyed. "I want to see!"

Callum suddenly shrugged. He lifted his hand and Holly turned the page.

"Wow. It's here. I mean it's this room. You did know that?" Her finger, drifting just above the old paper, indicated the fireplace, and the position of the window.

"So it is."

Holly carefully touched the weighty table legs of the workbench, then the bowls of herbs.

"That's rosemary. That one – I'm not sure. Hawthorne would love this..."

128

"Actually, I'm sure she'd be quite wary," Callum remarked.

Holly stared thoughtfully at the figure of Doctor Sliddery. "His face is really strange – at first you think it's quite a nice face, sort of scholarly, then you see other things in it - "

Callum pulled on her arm, but she resisted.

Then she felt her heart speed up. The room began to pour into the page, the scent of herbs suddenly thick and overwhelming. Holly felt a queasy darkness overtaking her. She stared at her feet, and slowly her head cleared.

She realised Callum was still standing beside her. She noticed the carpet had gone.

Then she looked up. Doctor Sliddery was straightening up from his workbench. He pushed back his chair with one hand. In the other he still held a long, black quill. The chair scraped loudly on the shining oak floor.

Apart from the ponderous tick of a grandfather clock in the corner, there was no other sound.

Holly felt Callum squeeze her arm warningly, then let go. He continued to hold his hand out, awkwardly, in mid air. Holly stood perfectly still.

Doctor Sliddery was wearing a long dark green robe over his coat and waistcoat. He pulled it more closely round himself as he surveyed the work on his desk. Holly noticed the robe was fur-lined. The room was extremely cold.

There was a faint tap at the door. Holly and Callum's eyes turned swiftly towards it. Doctor Sliddery ignored it. The door began to open, cautiously, and a thin child struggled round it, carrying, with difficulty, a heavy basket of logs.

"You are late." Doctor Sliddery spoke coldly, and without looking round. The child bobbed a nervous apology at his back, but did not speak, lugging the wood over to the fireplace.

Holly noticed odd streaks of white in her hair as she moved across the light from the window. The child's glance passed incuriously over Callum, then paused. She did not stop moving, but stared for a moment at Holly. Holly stiffened.

The child's eyes flickered, then she turned to her task, heaving the logs onto the hearthstone, and laying the fire.

Holly watched her, noticing the thinness of other girl's back and shoulders through her shabby dress, and as she knelt, the exposed bare soles of her feet, blackened with grime. She felt a deep pity, as though the other girl had told her how lonely she was.

It was hard not to shiver, it was so cold. The room seemed to darken for a moment. Doctor Sliddery had turned around.

"Tell me your age" he said to Holly, looking straight at her. His eyes were very blue, and glittered unpleasantly.

Holly heard herself gasp. "You can see me!" she said stupidly.

"I can see you." He was unsmiling. "I do not welcome strangers here. Those who enter this house do so at my bidding. Your age, if it please you to respond."

"I – I'm thirteen – I - " Holly felt pure animal fear rising inside her.

"Holly – the door – run - " she heard Callum hissing in her ear, and then she felt him pulling at her arm.

Somehow she moved her feet and turned to run. Callum was already halfway to the door.

"I think not."

Doctor Sliddery stepped swiftly and surely into Holly's path, and his hand closed around her upper arm like a trap. Across the fur-lined robe she glimpsed Callum as he wrenched open the door.

"Come on Holly!" he shouted, his back still turned as he disappeared from view. The heavy door swung slowly closed.

# 20    The Wood Breathing

Even as he felt the door close behind him, Callum realised Holly was not following him. His whole chest seemed to be pounding, and his legs felt shaky.

And he was not in the hall of No. 71.

He stood in a soft green dimness. Pine trees arched above him, their branches pungent with resin, their needles green on the trees and brown under his feet.

The trees were very still. All sound was deadened.

Ahead of him a faint path wound away between higher banks mounded in pine needles under the trees. He stared at it, unbelieving.

He turned around, and behind him was the door to the Gardening History Room.

He touched the doorknob, wonderingly.

Then he looked away down the path through the trees, and took a few steps, pausing with his hand on a rock outcrop softly coated with pine needles on every horizontal ledge. Callum had the most peculiar sense of the wood breathing, from dark, secret lungs.

No birds sang. There was not a breath of wind. There was no sign of life, except the wood itself. He lifted his hand and stared at the brown pine needles that clung to it.

Callum remembered Holly.

"Nothing for it," he said out loud, and heard his own voice in the quietness of the wood.

He turned back to the door, grasped the knob and turned it.

# 21    On The Top Step

"Do not struggle.  I will hurt you if you do."

Holly decided to obey.    Doctor Sliddery's hand remained clamped around her arm.  She was near enough to notice his smell, a mix of sharp sweat and damp, indoor mustiness.  Under her fear, she was still utterly amazed.

Doctor Sliddery twisted round to see the grandfather clock.  He wore his hair drawn back in a short pony tail and fastened with a dark ribbon.  It looked greasy.

"Already eleven of the clock."  His gaze turned to the thin child still crouching by the fire.  "So light it, girl!" he commanded.  Holly saw the child's hands tremble as she finished her work, and then she stood up, eyes downcast.

"Open the cellar door."  Doctor Sliddery jerked his head at the girl, and stepped out of the room into the hall. Holly scuttled alongside him, her arm hurting, whatever he'd said.  The thin girl hurried in front of them, and pulled open the small door in the hall.  Behind it a flight of stone steps led steeply downwards into deeper gloom.  The smell of damp rose in Holly's face.

"You said thirteen, girl?" Doctor Sliddery rounded suddenly on Holly. "Do you speak the truth?

His eyes were dark blue, even beautiful, but in colour and shape only. She stared back, taking in their cold glitter.

Anger quickened in them.

He shook her, and Holly gasped out, "Yes! Thirteen!" before she had time to decide whether to speak or not. He relaxed his grip. His face slackened for a moment, with something like relief.

"Wait down there then."

He thrust Holly forwards onto the top of the cellar steps.

"And you too" he said contemptuously to the thin child, who stepped obediently onto the step next to Holly, as he slammed the cellar door shut.

They heard him shoot the bolt.

The darkness seemed to be pressing on her face. Holly fought herself not to scream. She put out a shaky hand, and touched damp stone.

Then a warm, human hand touched her other wrist, and fingers crept into hers.

Holly drew a long, shaky breath. "Who are you? What's your name?"

There was a long silence.

135

Holly wondered if the thin girl could talk at all. Perhaps that was why she was a servant, almost a slave, it looked like, to this horrible man.

But then the girl spoke.

"He says I have nae name. They call me Sparrow."

"I'm Holly Berry." There was a brief pause. Holly faintly squeezed the hand. "What should we do?"

"Do?" the girl sounded puzzled.

"Can't we get out?" said Holly. "Or - isn't there any way we can make a light?"

"No" said the other girl simply.

Holly thought for a moment.

"Well we can keep each other warm. And we can sit down."

Keeping gentle hold of the girl's hand, she felt around for the edge of the step with her other hand. Then she sat carefully down. The child sat down beside her, and Holly, feeling the better for protecting someone else, took hold of the small hand with her other hand, and put her arm around the narrow shoulders.

The stone step struck cold through her jeans.

"My name is Holly," she repeated. It felt as if she should say something. "I live in this house too. But in a different time." She felt Sparrow's head turn towards her in the darkness.

"I live with Callum, and Liddy – and the house is a bookshop in my time. And Doctor Sliddery's book is kept in a glass case for people to look at."

"His book is finished, in your time?" Sparrow sounded quite astonished, as well she might, Holly reflected.

"Yes. Why do you live here Sparrow? Don't you want to run away?"

"Run away." Sparrow repeated the words.

"Don't you know someone who would help you?" Holly persisted. She felt Sparrow's thick hair touch her shoulder as the child shook her head.

"But when did you come here? Where is your family?"

Sparrow clutched Holly's hand tighter.

"I dinnae remember. Doctor Sliddery says my mother didnae want me."

There was a silence. Holly tried to think what to say.

"He says she didnae want me. Nae body wants me here. They're all feared of me. You're kind, Holly. But if I show you, you'll be feared of me too. "

Holly felt the hair rise on her neck, and her heart bumping.

But the little hand in hers was warm. Stan came suddenly into her mind, his broad grin, his faith in books and reason.

She took a breath, then said – "You have to face your fears. Why are they scared of you?"

The child took Holly's hand in both of hers. She found Holly's right hand index finger. Then she touched it to her own index finger on her own left hand. Then Holly's finger to her next finger. And the next. And the next.

And then the next. And then back to the thumb.

Holly sat still. Then she touched round the fingers again. Not four, but five. The child had an extra finger on her left hand.

"Now ye know. I bear the Mark. Minister Wormelow says sae. Doctor Sliddery took me in when none else would."

Holly sat still in the dark.

Then she hugged Sparrow to her. Sparrow let out a sob.

Time passed slowly. Once Holly persuaded Sparrow down to the foot of the stairs, but there was no sign of light coming from anywhere. By common consent, they were back on the top step, waiting for the door to be opened.

"What will he do when he comes back?" Holly worried. "Is there no-one else who might let us out if we banged on the door?"

"Lizzy'd not help us. She comes in by day to cook. She'd not stay in The Crow House at night, and she's feared of him too."

"The Crow House?" said Holly. She shuddered suddenly, without knowing why.

"Here. This is The Crow House. Tis its name," said Sparrow.

There was a short silence.

Then Holly asked, "Why's he so interested in how old I am?"

She felt Sparrow shiver.

"What?" she said to her.

"He's always after years" Sparrow said. "He has nae age at all of his ain. He takes his youth from ithers. He calls it the Gleaning. It's a part of his Darkment."

"I don't understand. What's Darkment?" said Holly.

"I mean he's bad, bad right through." The hand still holding Holly's tightened. "He'd tak' your youth away, for himself, if he can."

"But how? said Holly again.

"With the knife," said Sparrow. "He has the Darkment Knife."

Holly felt Sparrow's fingers close around her own hand, and lift her fingers again. This time she felt the flesh of Sparrow's arm. She felt the warm crook of the child's elbow. Sparrow made Holly's fingers touch several raised ridges of skin.

139

Holly realised that what she felt under her fingertips were scars.

"He did that to you?" She was appalled.

"Those are the years he's gleaned from me. I tellt ye," said Sparrow.

There was a sudden crash on the other side of the cellar door, as the bolt was yanked back.

Holly and Sparrow cried out as daylight flooded into their prison. They put their hands over their eyes, staggering to their feet, as they were pulled out into the hall.

# 22   Back at Home

As the door began to open, Callum turned his head to take one last quick look at the place where the hall should have been, at the pine wood, with its quiet winding path.

Then he took a deep breath, and stepped back through the doorway into the room he had just run out of.

But even as he closed the door behind him, he knew he was back at home. The warm summer sun shone on the bookshelves, and Doctor Sliddery's book lay open in the glass cabinet, whose lid was still raised, just as they'd left it.

He went towards it, and automatically closed the lid, turned the key and dropped it into the drawer below. Then the door burst open so suddenly that he leapt away from the cabinet, then froze.

Holly and the thin girl came stumbling in through the door, Doctor Sliddery gripping each of them by their shoulders as he forced them into the room.

# 23  A Child Weeping, Somewhere

Doctor Sliddery stared around him at the bookshelves, the tall window and the marble fireplace.  For a moment, Holly even saw him focus on the street outside.  No-one else moved.  A humourless smile curved his thin mouth.

To Holly's relief, he let go his grip on her shoulder, thrust Sparrow away from him.  He brushed his hands together fastidiously, and walked calmly across to the glass cabinet.  Everyone heard his swift intake of breath as he saw the book.

"My Herball" he said softly.

He looked up sharply and raked cold eyes over the three of them.  "You are none of you to move" he said.

Holly waited till he bent his head over the Herball again, then exchanged glances with Callum.  We're ok, but we need a plan, she thought hard, trying to communicate with him.  Callum just looked shocked.

Holly glanced sideways at Sparrow, and saw she looked simply terrified, staring round the room with no way at all of understanding where she was. Holly caught her eye for a moment and gave her a little smile, but Sparrow did not seem to notice.  Holly thought how strange, how wrong, Sparrow looked, with her white streaked hair and dirty bare feet, standing there in the warm, cheerful bookshop.

There was something awful, too, about the sight of Doctor Sliddery standing here, in Liddy's bookshop. Holly wondered anxiously what would happen if Alison or a customer came in. In some ways she desperately wished an adult would turn up and take charge. But could they?

Doctor Sliddery was staring down through the glass at the Grete Herball. He seemed full of admiration for his work. "It is well done," he murmured, "Truly, a work of scholarship, and most suitably displayed and bound."

He tried to open the cabinet.

Holly looked at Callum again.

Dr Sliddery looked up, annoyed.

"You" he said to Sparrow, "Where is the key?"

Sparrow let out a whimper. Doctor Sliddery gave a hiss of derision. "You are a poor creature, yet still not quite used up." He considered her speculatively. "There should yet be another gleaning."

"Leave Sparrow alone." Holly was shocked to hear her own voice. She thought of Stan, and stood her ground.

His gaze moved away from Sparrow. His mouth stretched as he laughed, though he made no sound. But when he spoke, his voice was soft with menace.

"You are stronger," he said. "You would even dare to tell me what to do. I would take a whip to you, to mend your manners."

Into Holly's mind came a picture of Hawthorne, who surely never used a whip. She took a step towards Doctor Sliddery.

143

She thought as hard as she could of Hawthorne.

She made herself look at Doctor Sliddery's dark blue eyes. She imagined the divining twig in her hands.

Somehow, she held his stare. She did not blink.

Very slowly Doctor Sliddery took a step back towards the door, and then another, backing so that he continued staring at Holly.

As he reached the door he turned contemptuously away, and as he did, he caught hold of Sparrow, gripping her tightly by the upper arm. Holly heard her wail as he yanked her through the doorway, and then they were gone.

The door shut with a snap.

"Bloody hell" said Callum.

"I feel sick," Holly said. She sat down suddenly on the rug and put her head in her hands.

They both stiffened as they heard first a muffled sob, and then more clearly, the sound of a child weeping, somewhere in the house, but far away.

# 24    She puts her faith in it

*She lies awake on the thin mattress, waiting for the moon to rise. She hears an owl hunting over the rooftops, and at last, through a gap in the sarking and a missing slate, sees a rim of silver moonlight which tells her it is time.*

*She adds a working man's jacket, shabby, too big, over the top of her other clothes, and carefully stows her Red in a pocket.*

*Silently, she feels her way down the wooden ladder that leads to the landing below, and gliding insubstantial as a ghost, she makes her way down the next flight of stairs. She clutches her Red to give her the courage to pass the room that Dr Sliddery sleeps in, but then she is past his door and hurrying down the last flight of stairs. She flies past the stained glass window, its vibrant blue border dimmed to silver in the moonlight.*

*Grateful for once that no other servants will stay the night in this house, she reaches the back door.*

*For many long moments she works the bolt back, flinching at every small sound. At last she slides round the door and as silently closes it again.*

Stealing through the West Port she turns down Agnew Crescent and into Lilico Street, skirts the new manse and makes for the Inks, where the tinklers have been encamped.

It is only when she has crossed the Inks, and is standing by the ruins of the castle that she finally admits to herself that they have gone. The first birds have begun their dawn chorus.

Sparrow squats on a stone, and hugs herself, rocking forwards and backwards.

She is still there, chilled to the bone, four hours later, when the minister takes his morning walk along the Inks. Mr Wormelow loses no time in scolding the runaway and returning her to No. 71 North Main Street.

Doctor Sliddery thanks the minister for his trouble, and locks Sparrow in the cellar for the rest of that day.

The next day, she begins to collect broken glass, prising it from the midden by the back wall of the garden, the place where generations of servants and women of the house have thrown out their smashed pots and bottles.

She selects her shards of glass carefully from among the debris. Green, glinting and jagged. She puts her faith in it.

Day by day she stores it, in increasingly large quantities, in an old tea crate hidden behind the comfrey patch.

146

# 25  It is Not Always
## What it Seems

Good news is shop may have buyer bad news still stuck here. Deeply relieved you and Callum now speaking u r a star.  Dad xxx

Holly hung around the kitchen, waiting for Callum.

"He really can't get up in the morning" she complained to Liddy.  Liddy cupped her hands round her mug of coffee and smiled.  Holly flicked open her phone and read Stan's message again.  Then she texted back:

Sell it quick. xxx

She peered out at the day.  The sky was soft and grey, uncertain whether to burn off or settle into drizzle. Unsatisfied, she turned back to Liddy.

"Dad says he thinks he might have a buyer for our shop in Carlisle."

"That's good news" said Liddy.  "It'll be good to have him back here in Wigtown.  Did he say if he can get over to visit?"

Holly wondered if Liddy really knew already.

"Didn't say," she said.  "Soon, I hope."

147

She glanced down. "I'm ok, you know, about – you and him" she added, her eyes on her phone. She shut it down.

Liddy stood up, walked round to Holly's side of the table, and held out her hand. Holly smiled uncertainly for a moment, then squeezed it briefly before letting go.

"He didn't actually say if he was likely to get over here though" Liddy said, "I wasn't messing about. I really don't know, but I thought you might."

"It's fine, don't worry," said Holly, and sighed, as Callum tottered round the door, rubbing his eyes and making groaning noises.


After her breakfast Liddy rushed off to let in Mr Drouth, and Holly, seeing Callum about to refill his bowl with cereal, lifted the packet and held on to it.

"Callum" she said.

He glared at her. "I need my food."

"I just want you to wake up and listen." She handed him the cornflakes. "Ok? It's important. I can't get the sound of Sparrow crying out of my head. It was horrible. I really hate the idea of her crying in this house."

"Well she isn't doing it now," he said, sloshing milk over a brimming bowl.

"No, well, I suppose we heard her because the two times – centuries or whatever - were just – sliding across, or whatever they do. But it was awful."

Callum munched, but looked up at her briefly. "Ok, it was."

"Well, you know what I told you, about the Gleaning. What Sparrow told me when we were shut in the cellar. About how Doctor Sliddery steals years from her so he doesn't get any older. And that awful knife he uses on her. Sparrow had some weird word for it. Darkment, I think she said. His Darkment Knife. Sounds scary. I can't stop thinking about it." Holly paused. "I can't help wondering if that's why Sparrow looks so – small. And what about her hair?"

"The white bit?" Callum re-loaded his spoon. "Mmm. Worries me too."

"Well, the thing is," Holly continued, "I can't think of anyone to talk to about her except Hawthorne."

"Hawthorne! What can she do? Doctor Sliddery's not going to listen to her. He probably thinks she's scum."

"Um. Well, I know. But I think she's the only person who can help. What else can we do?"

"Perhaps we can't do anything." Callum put down his spoon. "Who was supposed to look out for children back then?"

"Well, I dunno. The church? But I met the minister once when I was with Hawthorne and he was slimy. He's called Mr Wormelow."

"Good name for burying people" Callum observed.

Holly giggled. "True. Anyway, I still can't think of anyone who seems trustworthy, except Hawthorne."

Callum continued to look at Holly. He munched, swallowed and spoke.

149

"But Holly, as I said before, who is Hawthorne really? I mean -" he held up his spoon to still Holly's indignant protest " – what do we really know about her? What kind of – reputation has she got in Wigtown? Ok, I agree she seems alright, but you can guess what some of those Wigtown people *then* probably call her. Starting with Mr Wormelow, from what you said."

Holly looked at him, hopes dwindling.

"Mind you," he said "I haven't got a better idea."

"Right then" Holly pulled herself together. "That's what we'll do then. We'll take Drum to the wood today."

"Ok. But before that," said Callum, "I want to just walk round here and, er, check some doors." He looked up from his bowl.

"It freaked me, going through that door and finding a wood. Of all things. Just want to make sure it's not still hanging around."


So after Callum had dumped his cereal bowl in the sink, they set off to the Gardening History Room and tried walking through the door, first in one direction, then the other. And then the cellar door and all the doors on the first floor and finally the attic too.


No amount of opening and closing of any of the doors created anything surprising.

Coming out through the café with Drum's tack half an hour later, Holly heard Mr Drouth expounding to Liddy.

"...you would of course be doing me the most tremendous favour, my dear Liddy, but all in the advancement of knowledge, you know – ha –"

They were standing in the doorway of the Gardening History Room. Holly and Callum paused in the hall, behind Liddy.

"Well, my instincts are to say no" said Liddy, but she looked uncertain.

"My dear Liddy, I do understand" said Mr Drouth, a pleased smile lighting his neat small features. "But you are to have ab-so-lutely no worries! I have here a letter - " he produced it with a flourish from his inside jacket pocket " – of recommendation from the National Library of Scotland. Our colleagues there are adamant that in an ideal world The Grete Herball should be fully scientifically examined – parchment, inks, all the data – but as I do have – ha – strings to pull" he chuckled modestly "- your marvellous old book can be there today, and back here the day after tomorrow. Now where can there be a problem in that?"

Liddy looked at him. "Could I just see that letter?"

Mr Drouth extended it to her with a little bow.

"Ok" said Liddy, after a pause. "I'll just give this person" she waved the letter, "a ring. You understand, I have to check." She beamed suddenly and charmingly on Mr Drouth, fluttered the letter and disappeared behind the "Private" sign.

151

There was a little pause. Holly and Callum exchanged glances. Mr Drouth straightened his cuffs.

"Well you can't be too careful" said Callum darkly. He stalked out through the front door of the shop without looking at Mr Drouth.

Holly gave Mr Drouth a tight, uncomfortable smile, and followed Callum out.

After a single but cunning attempt to dodge Holly as she reached to put the halter rope round his neck, Drum seemed to resign himself to the prospect of work. His tongue worked his single pony nut busily while Holly and Callum gave him a rather quick brushing and tacked him up.

"Do you want to ride him today?" Holly asked Callum politely.

He grinned. "It's ok, my bike has a nicer temperament. You can have him."

They set off along the lane.

"You know I haven't" - Holly saw Callum slowing down to speak to her – "felt quite comfortable going through doors at home since I stepped out of Doctor Sliddery's room straight into a silent pine forest." He scowled over the handlebars. "It was freaky."

"Didn't you think about following the path, finding out where it went?" enquired Holly, pushing Drum into a reluctant trot to stay level with the bike.

"You must be kidding. It was not an inviting sort of wood."

"Why do you think Sparrow calls it The Crow House?" said Holly.

Callum breathed out and pressed down on the pedals.

"Hate to think."

A woodpigeon cooed. The air was cool and soft, the warmth of the sun beginning to strike through Holly's sweatshirt. The hills on the other side of Wigtown Bay began to emerge through fraying streamers of cloud and mist. Drum cheered up and trotted faster.

"You are lucky" Holly called back over Drum's trot, "It's so nice here."

"Who's lucky? I thought you were moving in with us."

Holly turned anxiously in the saddle to see him, but he grinned, and then bent his head over his handlebars to catch up.


Drum nosed his way through the hawthorn bushes to the hurdles, and whickered before stepping strongly through. Callum abandoned the bike at the edge of the stubble before the bushes began and followed Drum through the gap.

Holly saw a woman kneeling beside the fire, deftly flicking oatcakes over on a griddle suspended under the tripod. But it was not Hawthorne.

Callum noticed at the same moment, and caught Holly's arm. But Drum whickered again, and the girl by the griddle stood swiftly up and turned round. It was Ana.

"Good day to you" Ana said in her soft, accented voice. "Come, eat with us."

The very old, toothless man from the dancing at the market was crawling slowly out from Hawthorne's bender, followed by another man, who was short and thickset as he stood upright, but powerful, in the prime of life.

"This my father, Zennor" Ana nodded at the toothless man, who gave Holly and Callum a broad, gummy smile, and nodded his head several times. She ignored the other man until her father spoke rapidly to her in their own language. Ana tossed her head, then said, "And this Tomas." She hitched a slim shoulder briefly in the direction of the other man, who did not smile.

Holly and Callum tethered Drum to a branch and loosened his girths, then took a seat in the grass around the fire. It seemed to be a very early morning in Hawthorne's wood, and chilly. They huddled as close to the fire as they dared.

"Good day everybody" Holly said awkwardly. "Er, why are you using Hawthorne's ...I mean where is Hawthorne?"

Zennor looked helplessly at Ana, who made a gesture of impatience, and translated. Then she turned back to Holly.

"Hawthorne is on journey today. She back tomorrow. We are her friends, we keep her place safe."

"Oh. Good." Callum managed. Ana slid some fragrant oatcakes neatly off the griddle onto tin plates and placed one on the ground between Callum and Holly.

"Thanks" said Holly.

Callum picked one up and passed it quickly from one hand to the other, blowing on it.

"You want see Hawthorne, yes? Is important?" Ana said, "I am Hawthorne friend, you trust me."

Holly glanced at Callum, trying to think how much to say, trying to remember what Ana and the Ursari already knew. Were they really looking after Hawthorne's camp?

Callum gave her a cautious nod.

Holly said carefully, "It's about the little girl. The one called Sparrow, who lives in Doctor Sliddery's house."

At Sliddery's name, Zennor stiffened and began to babble, his eyes anxious. He crossed himself, touching his forehead, then his chest, then left shoulder and right shoulder, and then he did it all over again.

Holly saw the other man, Tomas, give him a swift, contemptuous look.

Ana reached out and gently took her father's hand in her own to stop his movements. She turned her dark eyes on Holly.

"Sparrow. I meet with her. She is his victim, just like to my aunt. Was my mother's little sister. Doctor Sliddery he steal her for the Gleaning, was twenty years ago. He make her old, so he stay young. He use her up and she die. Now he do the same to Sparrow."

"That's what we thought! Well something like that," said Holly. "But someone should try to save Sparrow. She's so scared. It's terrible."

She looked hopefully at Ana. "Can't we do something to help her?"

155

Ana turned her huge black eyes to Holly and gave her a long, straight look. "You not betray us? You promise on your mother life?"

"My mother's dead," said Holly, startled.

"My mother's isn't. We promise not to betray you on – on my mother's life" said Callum abruptly.

Holly looked at him. She was aware of all their eyes on her. She paused. Then she said, "Yes, me too."

Ana turned her head and spat neatly, catlike, onto the earth.

Then she said, her voice low, "We the Ursari, we come here to kill Doctor Sliddery. For revenge."

Tomas, the thickset man, burst into speech, and he and Ana argued briefly but fiercely in their own language. At last he stopped, shaking his head, shrugging.

Ana said, "He not like I tell you. But I tell him is necessary, I tell him you help us by help Sparrow."

"Oh" said Holly. She looked quickly at Callum. He looked pale.

"But what can we do?" he asked Ana, "We're only kids."

Ana looked puzzled. "Only keeds?"

"We're too young" Callum said, looking very young and anxious.

Holly rushed in.

"He's right Ana, we don't know how to - help kill - anyone."

"But you want save Sparrow, no? How if we find Doctor Sliddery and you save Sparrow, all happen same time. That way Sparrow safe, she not get hurt or scared, and
156

then you bring her to us, bring her here to Hawthorne wood. Is best. She best with the Ursari."

Ana smiled dazzlingly on them.

Callum gazed back, bewitched.

Holly looked impatiently at him, then back at Ana. "But how will this ever work? We can't all walk up to his front door together."

Ana pressed her hands together, and then her gaze moved quickly beyond them, away from the fire.

Zennor's eyes flickered between his daughter and Holly and Callum. Tomas, squatting by the fire, stared down at his knees.

Holly caught a faint sound as a young man stepped lightly out from among the birches. She saw it was Lev, the musician. He paused warily, his eyes on Ana.

Everyone looked round and Tomas sprang to his feet, his face angry.

Ana greeted him calmly and waved at him to come and join everyone else around the fire. Holly could see that Tomas was not at all happy about this.

Lev moved in next to Holly and Callum and squatted on his heels. He turned his face to catch their eyes, and smiled.

"You are safe, then. That pony, he got you away safe from the bear after all." His teeth were very white in his dark, handsome face.

Ana began to speak quickly in her own language to the group of tinklers. It clearly involved Holly and Callum because she kept glancing at them, and gesturing. Lev listened and smiled, where Tomas scowled.

"What have we let ourselves in for?" muttered Callum in Holly's ear.

"I know" she whispered back. "But what about Sparrow?"

"True," he said.

Ana suddenly turned back to them. "We talk it through, and we agree, you can help us by save Sparrow. It is we, who will do – the other thing. But we do not go in his house, he is too powerful in house. We send him message, he come to us. When he leave his house to come to us, you go there, save Sparrow."

Callum looked at her. "But when are you going to do this?"

Ana glanced briefly at Lev. "We do tomorrow night. At sunset."

"But we can't stay here till then! Liddy – I mean, our mother will miss us!" cried Holly.

"She's right, we can't" said Callum. "Can't you give us a signal, or something?"

Ana looked steadily at them, and then reached down into the grass, and picked two daisies.

She held out one to Holly, and when she took it, Ana put the other daisy in her own pocket.

"When petals fall, is time."

158

"Are you sure that will work?" said Callum.

"Thank you Ana" said Holly, ignoring him.

Ana's brilliant smile suddenly lit her face.

"Thank you so much! You are do what is right." She reached out, took hold of Holly's shoulders and kissed her cheek. Holly hugged her back.

For a moment she saw Callum lean forwards too, then he flushed and stared at his feet.

Ana smiled at him, and then glanced mischievously sidelong at Lev.

Tomas scowled again.

"You – go – now" he growled. "Not fail – or -"

Holly and Callum scrambled to their feet.

Lev stood up and put a long arm around each of Holly and Callum's shoulders. "You will do very well, do not fear, do not worry..."

He walked them back to where Drum was tethered.

"Look well about you in The Crow House. It is not always what it seems" he warned them. "And do not mind Tomas. He is jealous." He grinned and his eyes were laughing and light-hearted.

Drum seemed tired on the way home. The early sun had faded again and they all plodded back in light summer drizzle. It still seemed much warmer than the wood they had just left.

"What time is it this time?" Callum asked.

Holly looked at her watch. "We're in luck" she said, "It's still only two o'clock. I remembered to take a piece of thyme in my pocket. Hawthorne said it would help. Where's the daisy?"

She scrabbled through her pockets, and discovered it.

"I'm going to wrap it up, keep it from getting squished." She paused, staring into the hedgerow, and then picked off a dock leaf, and folded it round the daisy. She put it back in her pocket.

"I really can't believe" said Callum, "that it all depends on us being tipped off by a daisy. And that we're now accessories to a murder plot. And that our conspirators are relying on us to organise a kidnap too.

"But we have to" said Holly simply.

# 26   The Stone Fire

*The knob turns, slowly.  She steps into the room and then turns to drag a ragged bundle through the doorway. Her widened eyes check quickly that the room is empty.*

*Then she pays attention to closing the door, cautiously releasing the knob so the bolt slips noiselessly into its keeper.*

*She bends and gathers up her bundle.  It is heavy, and awkward, its folds of tattered cloth threatening to give way at any moment, and she locks her jaw with the effort of getting it across to the hearth.  Her feet are bare, and filthy. She lowers her bundle, still careful to make no sound.*

*There is the  ponderous tick of a grandfather clock, but otherwise the silence is complete and blanketing.*

*The large room seems to her to be waiting.  She feels its innate treachery.  It has let her in, and now its carved cornices, its fine rugs, its lighted candles, and most of all its fearsome bookcases, seem alert to her actions.  Perhaps it is giving the nod to what she is about to do.  Perhaps it will betray her.*

*She sets to work, ignoring the dull gleam of brass fire irons on the broad marble hearth. Instead she uses her hands to scoop the ashes out of the fireplace. Fragrant wood ash fans into the air as she works, and she bites her lip sharply at the pain of still-hot embers. But there is no time to wait.*

*When the fireplace is roughly clear of ash, she turns back to her bundle. Grey-fingered, she works the knots loose, and spreads open the cloth.*

*Her pale lips move soundlessly as she goes about her task. First she lays the green thorn prunings. Their sap is sharp in her nostrils. She winces at their barbaric thorns, but she makes a thick layer of them in the fireplace. Then, using both hands, she gathers up the broken green glass from out of the cloth, and scatters it over the thorn prunings in glittering showers.*

*Suddenly the grandfather clock clicks and whirrs.*

*Sparrow jerks back on her heels in terror. Her fingers move automatically to the pocket in her dirty dress, and close tightly around her Red, for comfort.*

*The clock begins to boom out the hour, and nervously she returns to her task, now scattering round pebbles over the green thorn and green glass. Her hands are shaking.*

*All that is left in the bundle now are three wide, flat stones, of the kind favoured by drystone wallers. She raises the first in both hands, and listens. The clock has ceased*

162

*striking. She strains for the sound of hooves in the street, or his steps by the front door.*

*After a moment, she lays the first flat stone on the fire she has built. Then the second beside it, and then the third.*

*Squatting in her enemy's stronghold, she deliberately looses her hair and shakes it free so it falls thickly around her narrow shoulders. It is as dark and wiry as horsehair, except for the incongruous streak of white which falls from each of her temples. She feels small inside the hair, but its protective warmth and bulk give her courage.*

*She combs it with her fingers, rocking on her bent knees.*

*At last she speaks aloud, softly and with hatred, to the man who is even now riding in through the West Port at the end of North Main Street.*

*"A Stone Fire I lay for ye
Nae luck come through your door.
This cold hearth lay a curse on ye
And cold death make sure..."*

# 27    The Moony Track

There was no wind, and Holly floated easily in the sky above the trees. When she looked down at the ground, she could see the track alongside the wood, lit by dulled silver moonlight. Its wheel ruts struck sharp shadows. By contrast, the wood beside the track was dark and still.

Someone stepped out from under the canopy of the trees.

It was a woman, wearing long skirts, with a shawl wrapped closely round her strong shoulders. Another shawl covered her hair. She stood for a moment in the moonlight, with her back to Holly. The woman looked away down the track, along the undulating silvery line made by the grass that grew down the middle of it. Then she half turned her head, and in that movement Holly recognised Hawthorne Agnew.

As Hawthorne began to walk away along the track, a tall, slim black cat sprang lightly down from the stone dyke enclosing the fields opposite the wood. The cat bounded swiftly after Hawthorne, then slowed to pad at her heels.

Another cat stepped noiselessly out from the woodland edge, and caught them up. Two more cats bounded down from the top of a stone dyke as Hawthorne passed beside it, one of them brushing sinuously along her skirts.

The woman and her four black cats walked along the moony track towards Wigtown, and in her dream Holly watched them.

Floating above them she watched them walk up the place that would later be Fountainblue Terrace and through the old West Port under blank, sleeping windows. The tall, black trees in the centre of the Mercat place were still, but Holly knew they were filled with roosting crows. Holly turned in the air, and soared towards her own open bedroom window.

Hawthorne had stopped, and the cats had folded themselves around her feet. She was standing under the trees, and looking up at No. 71 North Main Street, where Holly was now watching from her bedroom window, still floating, holding a thick fold of the velvet curtains in each hand.

Holly woke with her heart pounding frighteningly. She struggled free of the duvet and sat up, feeling for the light switch with shaky fingers. When it was on, she sat still for a moment, hugging herself, remembering.   Then she flung back the duvet and swung out of bed.

She carefully drew back the edge of the curtain, hiding herself in its velvet folds to peer down into the street. Nothing stirred, though there was indeed a full moon.   To her relief, there were no tall trees. Holly stared harder.

Then she saw it.  A slim, long-legged black cat, walking quietly and purposefully away up the street, on its way back through the West Port.

# 28   We Need a Spare Time Machine

"Do you think it meant Hawthorne was looking for us?" Holly worried to Callum next morning. "I can't remember if it was Wigtown now or Wigtown then. Though I think the trees were there in the market place. Maybe it was a warning. Are black cats lucky, or not?"

Callum rolled his eyes over his mug of hot chocolate.

"As if there wasn't enough on, with us getting ready to stand by and do a kidnap while a murder takes place." He paused. "Well. Step this way for analysis. Do you really think Hawthorne's trying to tell us to think twice? If you believe in dreams."

Holly pulled at the edge of a nail. "I wish we knew what we should do. It might be our one chance to help Sparrow. I even feel a bit bad about Doctor Sliddery. I mean the Ursari being out to get him. If it was now then we would ring the police or something."

"He is evil though" said Callum. He reached for a piece of toast. "To be quite honest, the thought of a world which hasn't had a Doctor Sliddery in it for quite so long cheers me up no end."

"Well you definitely get the impression that nothing's going to stop the Ursari having a go at him. You have to remember they tame bears for a living. So I'm sure they'd still do it whether we helped them or not. Maybe the only difference is saving Sparrow." Holly paused for thought. "I think Ana really wants us to save Sparrow, don't you?"

"How's the daisy?"

Holly felt in her pocket and carefully extracted the daisy, wrapped in its dock leaf. She unfolded it and they stared at the flower.

"It looks a bit sad," said Callum. He buttered his toast.

"Still got all its petals though. And not going brown yet." Holly looked up. She wrapped up the daisy again, folding the dock leaf carefully round it. The phone began to ring by the till in the hall.

Callum took a large mouthful of toast then croaked, "Can you answer that phone? Mouth full -"

Holly glared at him, then got to her feet. She paused by the doorway as she heard Liddy on the stairs. The ringing stopped.

"Good morning! This is Good Garden Books here. What can I - "

A pause.

"Oh no! Poor Pete! His shop's been *what*?!"

Callum stopped chewing.

"Oh my God, I've never heard anything like it... What? ...the paperback shop too? Are you sure?"

They both listened intently.

"Right, I'm on my way, thanks for ringing me. I'll do whatever I can to help."

They heard the phone ding as she put it back down.


Liddy walked into the café. She looked shocked.

"Ma – what was all that about?" Callum scented drama.

Liddy was twisting her long red plait in one hand. "There's been a break-in up at Pete's – you know Holly, the big bookshop up the street. And apparently another one on the other side. I'm going up to Pete's now, he's a pal, see if there's anything I can do to help."

She looked round the cafe as if she had lost something, then turned to Callum.

"Could you wait here till Alison arrives? Clear up for me would you, don't leave it to her?"

"That's ok Liddy, no problem" Holly assured her. Callum nodded.

"See you shortly then" Liddy paused with her hand on the door. "Perhaps it's just as well The Grete Herball went off with Mr Drouth yesterday." She hurried out.


Callum stared after her. Holly stood up, and began to gather together the mugs to take them back to the kitchen.

"She looks really worried Callum. I guess you don't get many break-ins in Wigtown."

Callum gave her a scornful look. "Surprise, surprise, we don't."

"Okay. Sorry I spoke." Holly swept the mugs off the table and turned her back, heading for the kitchen.

"Holly."

She looked back. Callum stood and picked up breakfast bowls and spoons. "Sorry" he said.

They cleared the rest of the table without talking, and Callum wiped it with a dishcloth, which he chucked into the sink from the kitchen door afterwards.

They sat down.

"It's just always been hard, you know, for my ma." Callum stared down at the table. "I mean, she's had to do it all on her own. She just does work very hard. Wigtown doesn't need some nutter breaking into bookshops."

Holly wanted to point out that Liddy being with Stan now would help. She decided not to. Then she heard the front door open.

She leaned forward on her elbows, listening.

"Callum. There's Alison coming in. Let's see if she's heard about the break-ins."

It was immediately obvious that Alison had. She hurried into the café looking flustered and upset. "Oh how dreadful!"

She dumped her bag on a café table without seeming to see it.

"Have you two heard the news? It's really awful, I didn't think such a thing could happen here!"

170

"Have you just been at Pete's?" asked Callum, "Alison. What's going on?"

"Och, I've never just seen anything like it," Alison sank onto a chair. She did not let go of her bag. A strand of hair hung by her cheek, tumbled from her clip.

Holly looked round for the pot, then got up to fetch her a cup of coffee.

"What's going on Alison?" Callum repeated.

"I've just been in Pete's shop. Oh, it's dreadful, just the mess, and that poor man, all his years of work" said Alison.

"That's kind" she added to Holly, accepting the mug. She took a sip, then looked up at Callum.

"I think you ought to get along there too Callum, stay with your mam. I could see she was very anxious. Just everybody wants to lend a hand. The town's in shock. It's no good for anybody."

Holly looked across at Callum. He gave a jerk of his head towards the door and left the room.

Holly said, "We won't be long Alison", and followed him.


On the doorstep, she looked up the street and caught sight of Callum running up the pavement. He went into the largest bookshop higher up the street. Two more people followed him in. Holly set off in pursuit.

As she arrived by the windows of Pete's bookshop, Holly slithered to a halt. The display window seemed to be carpeted by shredded paper. Long jagged splinters of polished wood stuck out here and there. Holly could not

171

think what she was seeing. Her brain would not make sense of it.

She stepped in through the open door and turned to look again into the window space. Torn paper curled over her trainers. She shuffled her feet. She bent and picked up a piece.

It said "Lavendul".

She stared at it, then dropped it and picked up another piece. A picture. Glowing stamen waved from half of a dark pink rose. She bent again and took a small handful.

"rimula veris". "gitalis purpur".

Then a larger fragment, in black Roman type, with larger letters, (was it a heading?) "New Herbal".

Shocked, Holly recognised it.

It was the book – the one in Pete's big window. Into her mind came a picture of it as it had been – as big as a laptop, but thicker. It had had gold tooling on the leather binding, and thick creamy pages, propped open on a polished wood bookstand to display the glossy plates. Liddy had pointed it out once. Said it wasn't as old as the Grete Herball, but she would still like to give it house room or something. Had she said nineteenth century?

Wasn't it called -?

What was that smell?

She looked up.

A small group of people stood huddled together by the till on the other side of the room. They were talking in low voices and gazing around them. Holly saw Callum standing next to Liddy, who had put her arm around his shoulders. Callum looked younger than usual.

The smell was horrible.

There was a heap of blackened stuff in the middle of the room. Holly realised someone had built a fire out of books.

Charred paper was still sifting through the air.

A furious arm must have cleared whole shelves of books onto the floor, and then flung them around the room. Some books had been wrenched apart at the spine, then hurled.

Several people were comforting Pete.

Holly watched him shake his head in disbelief, again and again. "But you know I never heard a thing" he kept saying.

"The police are on their way" said someone behind Holly from the door.

"Whoever did this did much the same to the Paperback Emporium too," contributed the barman from the pub.

"Much damage?" enquired the newsagent.

The barman's voice sank with apparent embarrassment, "Not as bad as here."

There was a moment's silence in the bookshop. Holly didn't look at Pete.

Then the barman said, "You've had a bird in too, Pete." He bent and picked up a long black feather. Then he stepped forward and drew another one out from under the edge of a bookcase. "That was nae sparrow" he added drily.

Holly looked. After a moment she saw another feather, quite near her, sticking out from under the remains of the New Herbal in the window. It was long and black, with a thick quill.

She shuddered.

"Holly" said Liddy.

Holly looked over at Liddy and Callum and saw Liddy reach out her other arm towards her. Without thinking about it she stepped across the sea of ripped pages and went to Liddy. She felt Liddy's arm wrap around her shoulders. No-one said anything.

A little later, after the police had arrived, Liddy, Callum and Holly walked back down the Main Street to No. 71.

"There's nothing more we can do" Liddy had murmured to Holly and Callum, having given her details to the police and been warned, as another bookshop, to expect a visit.

"Poor Pete" said Liddy. "It's like – like someone just – just had a rage in that bookshop. They must be mad."

"I expect the police'll catch them" said Holly with more certainty than she felt. A thought occurred to her. "Did they steal from the till as well?"

"That's another odd thing" said Liddy, "Apparently not, not in either of the shops."

"Still, I'm sure they'll get caught" Holly was determined to be positive. "Whoever did it wasn't being careful to leave no evidence."

"Oh I think they left evidence," said Callum.

Holly glanced across at him sharply.

Liddy was sounding quite apologetic. "I'm so sorry you had to see us like that, Holly, in Pete's. Wigtown's not the sort of place where stuff like that happens. People will be feeling very shocked. And of course it's rather worrying..." her voice trailed off.

"Ma, you mustn't worry" said Callum. "We'll buy a young wolf and leave it in the shop at nights" he added, watching Liddy's face.

Liddy glanced up. They exchanged a grin. Callum pushed open the door of No. 71, holding it out for Liddy as he went. Holly followed.


In the cool white hall, with its tall doorways into book-lined rooms, calm and undamaged, Holly suddenly, fiercely, wanted Stan to be there.

She lagged behind Liddy and Callum. She stared down at the floor, blinking hard. She waited, angrily, for the lump in her throat to go away.

The day in Wigtown was disrupted.   Standing a little later on the front step of No. 71 Holly watched two police cars parked by the Mercat Cross.  Wigtown's wide, peaceable street was waiting, everyone's business on pause.  Will rang up to talk to Callum about it, and Holly retreated to her bedroom.

She sat down on the edge of her bed, feeling lonely.

Some minutes later she heard a tap at the door, and Callum put his head round.

"Wow" he said, "Never in the history of Wigtown. "

He walked in and sank onto a saggy armchair beside the tailor's dummy.

"Is your life always like this Holly?"

"Like what?"

"Do weird things happen round you on a day to day basis?" he said.

"No." Holly did not want to pursue this.

"Don't be stupid.  What's vandalism in bookshops got to do with me?"

Callum sighed. "Don't get all edgy.  Didn't you get what I meant about someone leaving evidence?"

Holly felt impatient, out of sorts.  "How could I?  That's a job for the police."

Callum squirmed on his chair and hitched up his t-shirt to extract something from the back pocket of his jeans.

176

He laid the long black feather on the floorboards between them. It was only slightly bent from its time in his pocket. It lay on the wood, glossy, and somehow malevolent.

Holly glared at him. "So it's a feather" she said coldly.

Callum sighed. "It's not any old feather. It's a crow feather." He suddenly reached and kicked at it on the floor with his trainer. "Oh call me stupid, but the only person round here who seems to have a bit of a thing going with crows is Doctor Sliddery."

Holly laughed out loud. "What! You think a – a – supernatural vandal did for Pete's shop! And what crows?"

Callum rubbed at an eye with the back of his hand. "Come on, Holly. The Crow House? And I saw a crow hopping round him when he turned up at the market, you know, when we first saw the tinklers."

He looked earnestly at Holly. "Then think. You were there too. In Doctor Sliddery's study I mean. When he got up from the bench he was holding one like this." Callum indicated the black feather still lying on the floor. "He must use them to write with. And, here's a no-brainer - does Doctor Sliddery want The Grete Herball or not? Perhaps he couldn't find it cos Mr Drouth's gone off with it, and then he lost his rag!"

"But how did he get here? And why didn't he trash Liddy's shop too?"

Callum's shoulders sagged. "I dunno. Just an idea. Somebody really did for Pete's New Herbal though. And –

get this – you dreamed about crows in the tall trees, didn't you? You told me. "

Holly looked at him unhappily.

"And Doctor Sliddery spooks me," Callum went on. "Makes me think of crows, somehow, anyway."

"I can't argue with that" said Holly. They both looked down again at the feather.

"Have you checked the daisy since before?" said Callum, after a pause.

Holly dug in her pocket and withdrew the folded dock leaf. She unwrapped the daisy again, then froze.

"Callum. Look!"

She held out the daisy again.

A single petal lay beside the flower in the palm of her hand. As they watched, another white petal slowly curled and then dropped from the pinkish centre of the flower. And then, gradually, another.

Her heart started beating faster.

"Uh-oh" said Callum.

"Now what?" said Holly. She looked anxiously at Callum, and then folded her hand over the daisy as Liddy's footsteps came down the landing.

Callum got quickly up and went out of the door. Holly heard him talking to Liddy on the landing.

Nervously she re-wrapped the daisy, pocketed it, and went to stand by the window. She watched a policeman walking back from Pete's bookshop, talking into his mobile.

178

Wigtown people peered from windows, or stood talking in islanded groups.

Holly thought about Ana, and what she must be planning to do, now, centuries away. If she closed her eyes she saw the daisy again, its petals coming off. Her heart still thumped. She couldn't work it out.

"No Grete Herball" she thought. "How do we get into Doctor Sliddery's study without it?" And where was Sparrow now?

The bedroom door opened suddenly, and Callum came in, shutting it carefully behind him.

"We need a spare time machine" he said urgently.

"I know. I can't think how."

"What about Drum?"

"But we have to go all the way to Hawthorne's wood with Drum, then back to Wigtown." Holly objected.

"Well at least it'll be the right century" Callum said, "It's just a long walk."

Five minutes later they were hurrying down past the County Building. Callum pushed his bike. Drum's saddle swayed on the handlebars. "We're just going out," Callum mouthed at Liddy, as she stood talking earnestly to Alison and a young policewoman whose job it was to check details of every bookshop in the Book Town. Liddy looked very

179

preoccupied, but she put up a thumb to them, and that was that.

When they arrived Drum was resting a hind leg, hoof tilted, his head drooping, eyelids lowered, dreaming in the sunshine. Once tacked up, he was not much livelier, and Holly had to kick him to trot beside Callum's bicycle.

It seemed to take a long time to reach Hawthorne's wood, but to Holly's relief the hazel hurdles were still behind the bushes. She lay flat on Drum's neck, feeling leaves brushing her hair, as the pony heaved himself through the gap with a profound sigh.

There was no-one there, and in Hawthorne's wood the sun was just setting. A breeze gusted every now and then through the wood.

"They must have gone already." Holly slid anxiously off Drum.

Callum went across to the fire and put out a cautious hand to the ashes.

"Still warm though."

"Best get going then" said Holly, more firmly than she really felt about the next stage in their involvement.

She hesitated. "What shall we do with Drum? I did bring his halter."

"Oh, stick it on him and let's take him" Callum said, "though we aren't supposed to both ride him at once. Ma says his age should be respected. And I suppose we'll have to hide him when we get to Wigtown. Or tie him up in the pend and hope no-one sees him." He looked at Drum, who was tearing up spring grass as if he hadn't eaten in weeks. "Some getaway vehicle."

They took it in turns to ride on Drum, and at a slow, frequently interrupted trot drew nearer to Wigtown. The light faded until they were moving through a cool blue dusk. Their eyes adapted to the dim outlines of the track in front of them.

Callum pulled up Drum and dropped awkwardly to the ground. Holly scrambled up. They went on.

"This is Scotland with no cars" said Holly. She made her voice just loud enough to be heard over the evening birdsong, the rhythm of Drum's trotting hooves and the squeak of the saddle.

"I know – it's so – quiet – except for – birds -" Callum panted, jogging just behind her stirrup. "I can smell – woodsmoke."

"Nearly there then." A blackbird let out its staccato warning cry nearby and she heard it fly swiftly away through the hedge. Then they were at the foot of Fountainblue hill.

Drum dropped heavily back into a walk. Holly slid off and waited a moment for Callum to catch up.

"Shall we - take him up?" Callum was still out of breath.

"I just thought. If we take him any further, everyone in Wigtown will hear his shoes on the cobbles" Holly said. They led the pony off the track into a scrubby coppice and loosened his girths. Holly tethered him securely to a branch with the rope halter. Drum tugged once, then took a mouthful of leaves.

Holly's stomach sank nervously. She could hardly see Callum now. He looked young and slight in the dimness.

"This is it then" she said. "I wonder where the Ursari are? And Doctor Sliddery. And how are we going to get into the house?"

"No idea" said Callum. "You can be boss."

"Oh thanks."

They set off up the last hill into Wigtown. The cottages seemed eerily quiet, shuttered against the night. Scarcely any sign of light showed.

Once a small child cried, otherwise the town was very quiet. A half moon had risen.

Walking warily to one side of the road, they went through the West Port and past the Mercat Cross. It was darker still under the tall trees. Holly thought of hunched groups of roosting crows hidden in their newly leafed branches. It didn't make her feel any better.

Callum put out his hand and Holly stopped. Before them were the broad step and handsome columns of No. 71.

The wide front door was painted black. Holly stood on the step below it, feeling small. The thin moonlight picked out its familiar great brass doorknob.

She froze.

Because above it was a black doorknocker with a cruel curved beak and hard metal eyes. They watched her.

"Callum. The Crow House. Look."

He stood beside her.

"Oh fudge." He sounded shaken.

She stared at the doorknocker, trying to resist the sense that it was boring into her head.

Callum was pulling at her arm. When she looked round she saw he was pointing to a shuttered window. There was a slim chink of light showing where the shutters met inside the old glass.

Holly looked fearfully back at the doorknocker.

Then she stepped closer and peered over Callum's shoulder, through the chink between the shutters.

# 29    Take Heed Behind

All Holly could see was the smooth edges of the wooden shutters.  Callum was twisting his head from side to side, getting in her way, which didn't make it any easier.

"Can't see" he muttered.

"Let me look." Holly pushed past him, but try as she might there was no angle of vision through the tiny gap, only the shiver of candlelight.

"We'll just have to go for it.  At least by now the Ursari must have got Doctor S out of the way." Callum mumbled.

He turned back for the front door under the classical portico.

The moon had appeared now above the rooftops of South Main Street.  Holly found she was shaking slightly. She wanted to tell him to stop, but too late, he was trying the doorknob.

He turned his head and nodded at her urgently.

Oh bugger.

She set her foot on the step, and found she was following him, silently, through the open door into The Crow House.


Her eyes felt stretched as wide as they would go, but she could see nothing.  The hall was so dark she could not see her hand.  She lifted it right in front of her face, and found she could really see nothing. Panicking, she reached out and felt for Callum. He put his hand back and they clutched each other's fingers, standing still, clenched in the grip of ancient human terror of the dark.

A sound from the room on their left made their ears strain. Holly held her breath, so her ears had more chance to hear. Again, it came.

It was the sound of a man breathing, loud, ragged, a terrible sound, full of disturbance and fury.

Then a voice.

"She has even laid thorns, and broken glass."

His voice grated on Holly's ears.

"This I will not tolerate. Where is she?"

Holly's heart seemed to be crashing in her throat now.

Callum was dragging her away from the study door, up the hall to the foot of the stairs. They were still absolutely silent, some instinct for survival making each footstep light and wary.

There was a sharp click, and a whirring noise.

Callum's grip on Holly's hand increased painfully for a moment, then relaxed as the grandfather clock in Doctor Sliddery's study began to strike the hour. Under cover of the chiming they climbed the stairs to the first floor landing.

"It's him! Where the heck are the Ursari?" Callum muttered urgently.

"Something must have gone wrong."

185

"You can say that again. And what's he so mad about?" Callum's faint whisper sounded shaky now.

"How should I know? But we've still got to find Sparrow. Where on earth is she?"

"Higher up? Servants used to sleep under the roof didn't they? Shut up now, he might hear us" Callum whispered.

He began to feel his way along the landing. Holly followed closely and they began to climb the next flight of stairs, which had no carpet.

Below them, they heard a bell begin to ring, an impatient clonking.

Holly felt her insides clench with panic. She stopped on the stair and Callum bumped into her. She could feel him shaking. She tried to think.

"It's him. He must be calling Sparrow."


Callum pushed her on up the stairs, past the same doors that in the 21st century would become the doors of their own rooms.

"Maybe we'll meet her on her way down" he muttered. "Fudge. We should have thought to bring a torch."


She began to feel a little calmer as they climbed away from Doctor Sliddery. They reached the attic landing and stopped. Here there was a little thin moonlight coming through the landing window, and two closed doors.

"Shouldn't we try one of the attic rooms? She might be in one of them," Holly whispered.

"Wait. Listen."

They strained their ears. Nothing.

Then downstairs the bell clonked again.

She saw Callum turn to look at her, and nod, so she put her hand out to the nearest door and turned the knob.

The door swung slowly open.

The room was faintly lit. But it was not a room.

Holly saw a path winding away over pine needles between dark tree trunks and paler rock outcrops. There was only a very faint light.

Her nostrils filled with the resinous smell of the pines. She put her head through the doorway and looked sideways along the wall inside. The trees grew right up to it, and branches grew vigorously up to the door frame. But apart from that, there was no sign the pinewood was not completely natural.

She put out her hand and touched the solid grey-white painted door. She looked down and saw the toe of her trainer was already on the soft, pine needle strewn forest floor.

"Hell's biscuits – it's him, he's coming up the stairs!" hissed Callum from behind her, and he shoved Holly into the pine forest and turned to close the door at their backs.

"Callum – what are you doing?  We don't want to be in here - "

She stopped whispering as she too caught the sound of a step on the wooden stairs.   Callum held the door almost closed.

They froze.

They heard the footsteps come down the landing.

A pause.

Then Callum's eyes went to the doorknob he was holding.  He let go as if it had burnt him.

The door was yanked shut with a loud click.

They heard a key being inserted and turned.

All sense of what was outside the door vanished.  The silence in the wood seemed to grow.

"And what do we do now?"  Holly whispered.

"I really dunno."  Callum slowly lowered himself onto the edge of a rock cushioned by fallen pine needles.  "I've been here before though, remember?  But it wasn't through this door."

"Well you got out that time.  It feels a bit better in here than out there.  In a strange kind of way."  Holly sat beside him and looked around her in the quiet gloom of the forest. "Though I suppose most places feel better than Doctor Sliddery's house in the dark with him creeping through it trying to get us. But why did he shut the door and lock us in?"

Callum said nothing, and Holly continued, "Do you think he locked us in on purpose? I mean, do you think he knew we were in here?"

Callum heaved a sigh. "Dunno. Yes. Maybe. But we are locked in."

He peered into the gloom. "I don't know where the path goes. I came out through the door I went in by last time."

"I bet he did know we were there. Which isn't very comforting." said Holly.

She looked nervously back at the door, which was still a door, but from where they sat the walls seemed to fade into trees beside the door frame. She looked the other way, down the path into the trees. "I wonder what else is in here."

"Don't" said Callum shortly.

She thought back to a few moments before, when they were in the house. "I suppose we were too scared to be really quiet." She glanced at Callum, then stood up and took a step along the path. "Come on. We have to see where this path goes. There must be another way out."

"Why must there?" said Callum, but he got to his feet and followed her.

189

The quietness was eerie.  There was no wind, and no night sounds from among the trees, as there had been on the ride to Wigtown from Hawthorne's wood.

The path twisted between dark pines, and tended to descend.  They walked one behind the other, with Holly leading the way.

The softness of decomposing pine needles deadened each footfall.

Glancing to either side of her Holly could see only the dim shapes of more pines, and more, bristling columns of tree trunks that faded back into the dark.  Her head was filled with their thick, aromatic smell.


"Have we missed any turnings?" Holly whispered.

"Don't think so."

She hesitated, then went on, stepping carefully over tree roots, as the path wound downwards.


"Holly."

"What?"

"There's something behind us."

She stopped and looked round.  Callum's eyes were wide.  They listened.


"It's gone now" he said.

She strained her ears.

Nothing.

Callum nodded his head forwards along the path, and they went on.

Then she heard it too.

A soft soughing hiss, like a long intake of breath as something quested for a scent with its mouth open. And then a second sound was carried down to them from higher up, the sound of branches being pushed aside and snapping.

Callum and Holly stood side by side, frozen, listening.

A sharp gust of air made a branch beside Holly sway suddenly. Then another twig wafted. Without more warning than that, the wood surged suddenly in a strong breeze that gusted downhill towards them.

"Urgh! That smell!"

Holly was first to put her hands over her nose, but Callum almost instantly did the same. His eyes over the top of his fingers were appalled.

The warm, foetid reek of damp and rotting roiled down over them, insinuating itself easily between the trees. The stench was thick around them, as matted and solid as an ancient blanket, and Holly felt her stomach churn.

Callum grabbed her arm, and tugged her on down the path. She struggled after him, with her hair blowing over her face in the gusty wind.

And now they were running, gasping for breath, panic in their throats, desperately trying to outpace the reek, and whatever was coming behind.

Holly clawed her hair out of her eyes and strained to see the twisting path ahead. Callum ran in front of her, leaping and sliding as he tried to go faster without falling. From behind, her nervous ears caught again the sound of something big, and heavy, that was forging its way downhill through the thickly growing trees.

She rushed on, dry-mouthed with terror, feeling the whip of small branches, pushing herself off the occasional tall stones that flanked the path with her hands as she ran, feeling soft dead pine needles stick under her fingers.

They turned a sharp corner and without warning were forced to jump down a steep earth bank laced with tree roots. Someone was standing just ahead, a small figure, waving urgently.

"It's Sparrow!" Holly shrieked above the wind. She was so frightened she had nearly not recognised her. "Callum – stop!"

Just in front of her she saw Callum crash to a halt, saving himself from falling on Sparrow by clinging to a tree trunk.

Behind them in the stinking breeze, something moaned as if with hunger, and pressed itself through tearing branches higher up.

Sparrow beckoned urgently to them, turned and ran. They followed her as she led them quickly off the path between the trees, scurrying and ducking almost to ground level under the bare spiky branches that grew and bristled low down the tree trunks.

Without warning, Sparrow stopped and wheeled round. Surprised, and following as closely as they could, Holly and Callum nearly crashed into her, and then recoiled.

In one hand Sparrow was holding a long, black knife.

# 30    She Didn't Mean to Look Round

In the rotting stink and noise of the wind, Holly and Callum took a step backwards, eyes fixed on the knife, which shone darkly in Sparrow's hand.

Holly felt a desperate sob rise in her throat.

"No," said Sparrow, but they could barely hear her. She shook her head vigorously and then with all her force she stabbed the knife into a pine tree.

The knife stuck at a crude angle into the bark. Holly watched as drips of resin began to bubble from it.

Sparrow held the knife tight in her right hand, and put her six fingered hand on the tree, running her palm over the bark just below the knife still stuck out of the tree.

The wind rose to a howl, and as it filled ears they heard, over the top of the dreadful sighing, a snarl.

The thing that followed them had found the place where they had left the path. Holly heard it searching, felt it nosing at the trees, finding their scent.

"Quick, be quick," she heard Sparrow saying. But she stared back the way they'd come and saw something lunge into view. In the dim light, through the trees, she could not get a clear view of it, but for a second she took in the feathered height of its back as it smashed through the trees, and a scaly leg ending in a shining claw that embedded itself in the soft ground.

Holly began to run. In front of her the tree with the knife in it was paler. She saw Sparrow pressing on something that was now a dull grey-white, broadening in the gloom, spreading up and out, becoming panelled and chamfered.

Holly knew she was moving with all the speed she possessed, but it was like running through deep water in a slow and terrible dream. She saw Sparrow tugging and shoving at the tree, and suddenly she saw that now it was a door, and that Callum was stumbling through it, just in front of her.

She leapt forward, but her feet struggled through pine needles, branches caught hold of her, even the air seemed resinous and sticky. She didn't mean to look round, but she did, because the thing behind her shrieked, and she felt it breathing her in, and she saw its eye, high in the air but a snake's eye, amber like resin, reptilian.

And then at last everything speeded up. She was plunging through the door, banging her arm painfully on it, and Sparrow was dragging it shut behind the three of them.

Wherever they were, it was still dark.

Holly heard the unmistakeable sound of Sparrow turning a key in the door. The lock inside revolved and secured itself in the sudden, relief-filled silence.

"Oh, fudge," said Callum, in a very small voice.

Sparrow glanced swiftly at him, but said nothing.

Holly drew a shaky breath. "Oh God. Where are we now?"

She heard her own voice came out in a trembly whisper.

"Dinnae fear, Holly." Sparrow seemed more upright, her small shoulders bolder.

"We should be gone from here too, but it's nae sae bad as the Darkment."

Holly saw that the dim light in the room they had arrived in was coming through a small unshuttered window. Callum walked across to it.

"Holly" he said, keeping his voice very low, "you know what? After all that, you know, stuff, in the forest, all we've done is just come downstairs."

Holly stared wildly around her.

"This is still his house? Oh no!"

Sparrow surveyed them both. She took a tattered, reddish piece of cloth from a deep pocket in her ragged skirt, and wrapped it carefully around the knife. Then she put the bundle carefully back into her pocket. She looked up again at them.

"Time tae flit. I don't never want to come back here again."

She got them out of Doctor Sliddery's house through a labyrinth of sculleries and wash-houses behind the kitchen.

"No sign of these back at home. In our time, I mean", muttered Callum as they tiptoed past stone sinks and stacked wooden buckets through the gloom.

Callum let out a vast sigh as Sparrow silently closed the wash-house door, lowering its latch slowly with both hands.

Holly saw Callum turn solemnly to Sparrow. "Thanks. You know we came to rescue you?"

Holly had never seen Sparrow smile like that before. Her pointy face broadened suddenly in a wide, humorous grin.

Then she laid a finger on her lips, and set off through the cool, moonlit garden. They went out through the gate and turned into the pend. Sparrow paused under the arch between the houses and peered cautiously up and down North Main Street.

"Wait," said Holly, urgently. "You can't just – Sparrow, what was that place? How come you were there?"

"Yeah," Callum moved closer. "What was that *thing*?"

Sparrow stared at them. Then she looked down, and twisted her hands together.

"It was the Darkment. Doctor Sliddery's Darkment. He makes it. He makes it in his mind, when he's angry."

"But what was that awful – *thing* – that was following us?" Holly shuddered.

Sparrow shook her head. "I never want to find out," she said reasonably. "It never came so close before."

"So you have been there before," said Callum. "Why? And what's that knife?"

"Doctor Sliddery used to put me in the Darkment, when I was bad." Sparrow was almost whispering. "You can get out if you find a door."

"Well, yes, that happened to me too, once," Callum said. "But did he put you in the Darkment this time too? We didn't think he would be there."

Sparrow looked up. "This time I hid. And when I hid, turned out it was the Darkment. I had to hide because of the Stone Fire. But I stole his knife. I stole his Darkment Knife. He was never more angry. If he finds me now he'll kill me."

198

Holly tried to make sense of it all. "But there was no door to get out by. The *thing* – it nearly caught us. How did you know the knife would work, to let us out?"

"I didnae know," said Sparrow.

"What's a stone fire?" said Callum.

There was a silence.

Holly felt something lean onto her leg. She let out a stifled gasp and looked down.

A slim, long-legged black cat, faintly outlined in the moonlight, was winding itself around her ankles. It looked up at her, its eyes like mirrors. It was purring.

"Callum!" Holly pulled his arm to make him look. "It's Hawthorne's cat!"

My dream, she thought.

Sparrow looked swiftly down at the cat, then put out her hand. The cat rose gracefully on its hind legs and butted its head into her hand. Holly noticed suddenly that it was the six-fingered hand.

The cat turned right, out onto North Main Street, and then trotted purposefully away. A hundred yards away, it stopped and looked back.

Holly looked at Sparrow. They exchanged a slightly shy smile. Then Sparrow ran lightly after the cat.

"That's us then" said Callum, and set off at a trot. Holly followed him, keeping close to the line of the houses, and as much as she could, in the shadows, as they ran along North Main Street and downhill out of the town.

Drum whickered when he heard them struggling through the dark wood below Fountainblue hill to find him.

Holly thought she should be scared to be back in a wood, but this one felt so different. It smelled sweet with spring growth. She saw a fern half-unrolled in moonlight by a small dark pond. The tang of wild garlic wafted towards her.

They untied Drum, and led him back to the lane, where the black cat was sitting and neatly washing its face. Then it stretched, and set off again. Without discussing it, Holly, Callum and Sparrow followed on, leading the pony.

"We thought the Ursari were going to – er, get - Doctor Sliddery tonight," Callum said to Sparrow.

She looked at him, puzzled.

"I didnae see them. He went out, but before dark."

"You see," Holly felt she should try to clear things up, "Ana, and the Ursari, they told us they wanted to kill Doctor

Sliddery. Because of things he's done to them. So we wanted to make sure you were safe."

Sparrow just stared at her.

"So we came, but we didn't think Doctor Sliddery would be in the house." Holly paused, remembering. "But he was, and he was so angry."

Sparrow said, "I know why he was angered."

"Why?" said Holly and Callum both together.

"Because of I laid him the Stone Fire. I just said." She yanked Drum's head up as she walked, and glanced sideways at their puzzled faces. "T'is a curse. I cursed him. I cursed him to die a cold death."

They stared at her, speechless.

"How?" asked Holly, after a moment. "What do you mean?"

"I laid a Stone Fire in his hearth. It brings cold stone, cold glass and sharp thorns to his house. The next time he crosses his own threshold the ill luck takes him. He will die a cold death."

"But why -"

Sparrow turned suddenly towards them both, the moonlight catching her white streaked hair and thin face. "For because he is a thief!" Her eyes raged.

"For he steals years! He is old, too old to be alive! But he lives and others age, others die."

She walked on along the track beside them, silent now but breathing quickly.

201

Then Callum said, "Well I hope your curse works."

"It will" she said fiercely. She added, "And then I stole his Darkment knife."

"His what?" said Callum.

"His knife he uses for the Gleaning" said Sparrow impatiently.

Holly caught Callum's eye meaningfully, to remind him of her own time locked up in the cellar with Sparrow. But before anyone could speak, the cat, which had been trotting easily in front of them, paused, and let out a loud meow.

A woman stepped quietly out of the shadows to stand in the moonlight on the track. The slim black cat yowled again, and bounded towards her. Holly saw other cats winding around the woman's skirts and stepped forward eagerly.

"Hawthorne!" she called.

Callum looked round to see panic on Sparrow's face. He put out his hand towards her. "It's alright. She's a friend."

"Where is Ana? I want to see Ana. She promised, I thought you were taking me to Ana..."

"Honestly Sparrow, it's ok, we just don't know where Ana is at the moment, but I expect we'll find her in a minute..."

Hawthorne's calm voice came through the darkness. "Who have you there, Callum?"

She came closer, putting out a hand to turn Drum so that the moonlight fell on Sparrow's face.

Holly hovered nearby. "This is Sparrow -" she began.

Hawthorne's hand flew to her mouth.

Then she reached out both hands and took hold of Sparrow's, one in each. Sparrow stared at her in silence, and slowly allowed Hawthorne to turn over her left hand. Hawthorne held Sparrow's hand. Then she gently stroked the sixth finger. She stared down at it in silence for a moment.

Then she let out a cry like a sob, lifting her face up to the sky.

Sparrow froze.

Hawthorne sobbed again, then bent forward and stroked the child's thin cheek.

# 31    A Motherless Child

"Did you not guess she was mine?  My own daughter?"

Hawthorne was calm again now.

She smiled at Holly, the lines around her eyes crinkling. Sparrow slept with her head pillowed on Hawthorne's shoulder.

Still smiling at Holly, Hawthorne tightened her arm around Sparrow for a moment, and the child sighed, and burrowed closer.  She still clutched her Red.

Holly remembered how it had turned out that the Red had been Hawthorne's shawl, once.

They had walked back to Hawthorne's wood together, and now they were settled around her fire.  The blackened kettle dangled from the tripod over hot red embers.  The sky was still dark, but the first grey light was beginning to pale the east through the trees.

A blackbird started to sing somewhere in the leaves.

"To be honest, no."  Holly answered Hawthorne's question.  She glanced sideways at Callum.  He shook his head and shrugged.  The kettle began to sing.  Holly reached automatically for the horn cups which leaned at all directions in the grass. Their streaky sides gleamed in the firelight.

She looked again at Hawthorne's newly rediscovered daughter. It was nice for Sparrow. Not so nice for herself, though thinking this made her feel like a bad person.

She felt left out.

"Teabags?" said Callum to Hawthorne.

Hawthorne looked at him, puzzled.

Then she felt behind her with one hand, so as not to disturb Sparrow, and brought out from under the side of the bender a small pot with a lid.

Callum took it from her, lifted the lid and stared doubtfully at the dried, faded leaves within.

Holly bent over and sniffed. "It's lemon balm," she hissed.

Callum pulled a face, but the tea tasted refreshing, Holly thought, in the damp and chilly end of night in the wood. And the horn cup was warm and very smooth in her hands. She breathed in the lemony steam.

She was deeply relieved, though, that Hawthorne was back to normal. It had been scary seeing Hawthorne when she recognised Sparrow. Hawthorne had sobbed, making ugly, tearing sounds deep in her throat, and she'd dashed tears from her eyes with the back of her hand while she held Sparrow in both her arms as though Sparrow was about to run away. Which maybe she would have done, Holly thought.

Except at first she hadn't been able to, and then somehow Hawthorne had managed to speak, managed to make them all understand what was happening. How Sparrow, (who hadn't really been called Sparrow of course) had been snatched away when she was only four. How Hawthorne had waited, and searched, and begun to suspect, and returned to Wigtown.

It was all mixed up with the Ursari, of course, and what had happened to Ana's aunt. Hawthorne's eyes brimmed again, when she touched Sparrow's white streaked hair.

And it was all mixed up with herself, Holly Berry, and with Drum. And Liddy. And Callum.

Holly looked from Sparrow's streak of white hair to Hawthorne's quiet green-brown eyes. She saw that Hawthorne was nodding at her thoughts.

How does she know what I'm thinking, Holly wondered.

"Aye, I did need you, Holly Berry. When I saw how things had come together. A motherless child to save a motherless child. And I'm grateful."

Holly stared at her.

Drum, who she could hear tearing at the grass in his pen a few feet away, suddenly stopped. Holly felt the nervous thudding of his hooves go through the ground she sat on, and felt herself tense too.

A branch cracked somewhere close at hand.

Suddenly someone burst into the clearing. Holly and Callum sprang up, but as the intruder ran towards their fire Holly recognised Ana. Her black hair smoked loose behind her, she was out of breath and sobbing, and her eyes were frantic.

"Hawthorne!- Help me!- They have him – they have taken him!" She flung herself down at Hawthorne's feet, and clutched at her skirt hem with both hands.

Sparrow was awake and struggling upright, and Holly couldn't help noticing that Hawthorne took the time to look reassuringly at her lost daughter, and that she held onto her hand. Then she put out her other hand to Ana and spoke slowly to her.

"Ana. They have taken who?"

"Lev! They took Lev! And they beat him!"

Sobbing and still struggling for breath, Ana told her story.

"We send word, to Sliddery, to bring him to old Castle, near to by Ursari camp."

"So he did leave the house!" exclaimed Holly.

"But then he came back early" Callum muttered.

Ana drew a deep breath. "He come, but he come with priest Wormelow, and two militia men. He tell them - take Lev - and I run, and they catch Lev, and they beat him!"

"Then what?" demanded Callum.

"Then they drag him, away, back to Wigtown, I don't know!"

"But what about you? Didn't they try to catch you too?" Holly couldn't see how Ana could have escaped.

207

"Ha!" Ana threw back her head and gave a short bark of bitter laughter. "They need two militia men to hold Lev. And I am bear trainer. They careful with me! They just curse me, leave me." She glared at them all, her hands clasped tightly.

Holly looked at Callum, then Hawthorne.

"But where is Lev now?" asked Hawthorne.

"I do not know!" Ana burst out. "I am afraid what they do to him!" She pressed her face into her hands. Holly patted her arm gently, not knowing what else to do.

"He's probably in the Martyrs Cell," said Callum, unexpectedly. They all looked at him.

"In the County Building – I mean in the old Tollbooth." He looked at Hawthorne and Ana.

"It's under the modern County Building" he said to Holly, then added, obliquely, "School project."

"Oh!" Holly remembered the County Building, and the famous imprisoned Martyrs.

"Well done Callum" said Hawthorne. "I think you are right. That is where they would put him. He must be rescued."

"Yes! We rescue him! We do it now!" Ana struggled back to her feet.

Hawthorne gently let go of Sparrow, smiled down at her, and then also got up. She took hold of Ana by both hands.

208

"Ana. We will indeed save Lev. But you have run here from the Ursari camp. You have been frightened, and have not slept. First you must rest a little, and eat and drink. You are tired. Wait while I bring you food. Where are Tomas and Zennor?"

Ana shrugged and her shoulders sagged. "They are gone. I tried to stop them. But they say this place is unlucky for Ursari. They say Lev was not their clan and he did not bring luck either. They are afraid of militia men. They try to make me leave with them, but I do not. Tomas was so angry. But that is because I do not marry him." She looked up, and her eyes flashed. "I stay here and I marry Lev!"

Out of the corner of her eye, Holly saw Callum gazing open-mouthed at Ana.

Ana looked down. "But Zennor is my father. He so sad I would not go." A tear rolled, perfect as a golden bead of dew in the firelight, down Ana's smooth face.

Hawthorne reached out her hand and wiped away the tear gently. She brought food, and a horn cup filled with the lemon balm tea, and wrapped a shawl around Ana's shoulders. Sparrow moved and sat close to Ana.

Hawthorne crawled into the darkness of her bender. When she came back out into the firelight, straightening up slowly in the dewy grass, she was carrying her divining stick.

"Holly. You can help Lev now. You can find the best way to get him out of the cell." She held out the divining stick.

Holly shook her head. "With that? I don't understand. And why me?"

Hawthorne took Holly's hand and closed it gently but firmly around the divining stick. "You can use the stick to find more than water Holly."

She squatted back down by the fire, her eyes steady on Holly's. "In your hands, the stick will tell us the best way to find Lev, the best way to free him."

Holly was embarrassed. Also alarmed at the responsibility. But sneaking underneath was a faint but distinct pride that Hawthorne had chosen her for this task. Also, she had not the slightest idea what Hawthorne was talking about.

"How? What do I do? Why don't you do it?" she asked.

"So many questions." Hawthorne smiled imperturbably at her. "I ask you to do this Holly, because I know you can. And you would like to help to save Lev from Doctor Sliddery and Mr Wormelow."

Holly looked carefully at the ground.

"And," Hawthorne continued, "you do this by taking hold of the stick, and asking questions in your mind. You must be very clear about what you are asking, and then the stick will answer you. You must ask what the dangers are. And which way will be the best way. And which doors are locked. Let the pictures come into your mind."

Holly very briefly met Callum's eyes, and in them read his scepticism.

"Think about the Tollbooth" said Hawthorne.

"But I've only been in it very briefly" Holly said. "And in my time it doesn't look like that anymore."

"But the cell is still there. It's got an arched stone ceiling. Bolts on the door. You saw the door, Liddy said she took you in once," said Callum unexpectedly. "And it still has a window to the outside. You know, with bars on it."

Holly felt the stick in her fingers. The bark was smooth and dry, except for a little nub where a side branch must have been trimmed off. The cell door suddenly appeared in her mind, black painted metal, thick and weighty, with the bolts reaching right across it, and into massive keep rings on the wall.

"Ok" she said. "I'll try".

She thought about the County Buildings, trying to make them solid in her mind. She remembered the railings, and the noticeboards outside. She shook her head slightly. Try harder.

She pictured the stone cell with its arched ceiling. She was looking at the door from the inside, knowing the huge bolts were shot to on the outside. She tried being on the outside, but the bolts were huge, she was afraid she couldn't move them.

"Ask questions" urged Hawthorne, watching her.

Holly thought about the window. She tried to remember it. It was small, and square. It had bars across it.

211

A picture of Lev, bruised and dirty and alone, squatting on a hard plank in the cold cell, came into Holly's head. *Is he thinking about us?* she asked the stick.

And the stick was alive, unmistakably it shifted in her fingers.

She looked quickly up, met Hawthorne's gaze for a moment and smiled.

She went back to concentrating on the stick, and the cell. The bolts, she wondered. She slightly adjusted her hold on the stick, breathed, then addressed it in her mind.

*Is the door locked, or just bolted shut?*

Nothing.

Stupid, she thought suddenly. How could the stick answer that?

*Is the door locked?* she tried again.

Nothing.

*Is the door just bolted?*

She felt it just before the stick moved in her hand.

She was entranced.

*But can we – can I – open the bolts?*

In her hand the stick moved.

She took a deep breath, and concentrated.

*Do we – do we have to go now, to save him?*

The stick moved.

She looked up at the others.

They waited, silent and attentive to her. It was weird.

"It says we can do it" she said slowly. "Well, actually it said I could open the bolts on the door, because they're only pushed across, they don't have another lock on them.

"So all we have to do is distract the guard," said Callum cheerfully.

"Um. The guard. It didn't mention guards," said Holly. "But we have to do it now," she added.

"God's underpants," said Callum. "And what about Doctor Sliddery?"

Sparrow gave a sudden, harsh laugh. It was so unlike her that Holly stared.

"I cursed him. I cursed him to die," she said softly, and her eyes were on Hawthorne's face. "I cursed him with the Stone Fire."

Hawthorne stared at her daughter. Holly thought Hawthorne understood something more than she did herself. It was like watching someone get suddenly older.

They all got up, and made preparations to set off. Hawthorne called Drum over and caught him. Drum whickered and put his nose helpfully into Hawthorne's halter. She led him back, and addressed Callum.

"Who will be missing you Callum?"

"What?"

"Time has been passing Callum. Who will be looking for you?"

213

"Oh. Well, my ma, I suppose."

Holly, who was patting Drum under the warmth of his mane as she helped saddle him, felt a twinge of guilt. "Callum! We forgot. We've been out all night – here. Whatever time will it be at home by now?"

Callum was looking at Hawthorne. Now he did look worried.

Hawthorne looked from one to the other of them. "Callum, you must go home."

"But what about Holly? Can you imagine what ma's going to say if I turn up without Holly?"

Hawthorne sighed. "Holly has a task to do here. Lev's future maybe depends on her. I think it is you that has to go home now."

"But -" said Callum indignantly.

Holly heaved the girth up because Drum had just let out his breath. She felt a curious strength of purpose. "Callum. I have to stay to help with this. What about you say that I'm still out with Drum, but on my way home. You would have been quicker on the bike if we were on tarmac."

"That'll be really convincing if it's the middle of the night" Callum grumbled.

He wished them all good luck however, and Hawthorne and Holly went with him to the hazel hurdles.

He turned. "See you then Holly – soon – I hope, or else I'm history at home -"

He pushed his way out between the hazel hurdles.

"Keep hold of this," Hawthorne said, and Holly saw her put something into Callum's hand, and close his fingers over it. Callum ducked under some low branches, and disappeared from view.

# 32   Then the Light Went Out

Callum paused on the stubble, and looked back. The hazel hurdles were out of sight now behind the thick growth of hawthorn bushes. He carefully unfolded his fingers to see what Hawthorne had given him.

In the palm of his hand lay a sprig from some plant, with small, spiky, dark green leaves sprouting from each side of it. He sniffed it cautiously. It had a strong smell. He supposed it was thyme, because of what Holly had said. Ingenious. Witchy.

"Well let's hope it does something." He stuffed it into his jeans pocket.

It felt like late in the day. He hoped it wasn't the next day. The sun was low, and there was a lazy heat about the field. He looked around him for a moment. Then he ducked under a nearby bush and dragged out his bike.

His stomach kept rumbling as he cycled back up into Wigtown. Evening strollers greeted him. It was all very weird.

On the main street a lone police car was still parked outside Pete's. The front door of Good Garden Books was closed. Callum pushed the bike down through the pend and round to his back gate. There was no-one in the garden so he put the bike in the shed and went in through the conservatory door.

"Ma" he called. "Are you there - ?"

"Callum!" She was holding a phone. Very tense. Ah. Not good.

She said, "No – it's Ok, he's back – I'll kill him!"

She put the phone down and turned on him.

"Callum. Just what is going on?" She trained a fierce glare on him. Then (worse) she looked behind him. "Where's Holly?"

He tried to look cool and reassuring.

"Everything's fine ma. Holly's – um – on her way, just now."

She stared at him suspiciously.

"What's the latest on the break-ins?" he asked smoothly.

Liddy stared at him. Then she shrugged.

"Apparently it's all very baffling. There was no forced entry, you see. Just devastation within. So the police are questioning the shop owners."

She sighed.

"But people like Pete couldn't burn books. And if you were dishonest enough to try an insurance scam (and why would he, business is good) surely you'd remember not to bolt the doors on the inside. I just don't get it at all."

She looked sad. Callum went to her and gave her a hug.

"Don't worry ma."

Liddy hugged him back, but then held onto him and looked closely into his eyes.

"So. Where have you been? All day? I'd just begun to think I'd better really make the local police station's day and

217

report a double kidnapping as well. With pony." She obviously wasn't really joking, but he decided to pretend she was.

"Come on ma. What kind of masochist would kidnap Drum?" He recalled the unwilling progress Drum had made through the wood last night on the way to rescue Sparrow.

"I'm knackered" he added, genuinely.

His mother ignored this. She looked past him again.

"But Callum, where actually is Holly? I thought you said she was just coming in?"

Callum looked his mother in the eye, and lied.

"Drum was just being slow. I cycled on ahead to let you know we were on our way." He picked a scab on the back of his hand, casually. "Holly'll be down at the field, looking after him and stuff. Doing all the stuff you have to do when you put him back."

"Untack him, give him a pat and get back up here" said Liddy, looking narrowly at him.

"Well she doesn't have the bike, and she's got to carry the saddle. We thought it'd be best if I came ahead. She'll be a bit longer" said Callum inventively. "Anything to eat?" he added, hoping to distract her.

This seemed to work. He sank gratefully onto a kitchen chair and watched her open the Rayburn and lift out a casserole. A delicious smell wafted across the kitchen.

"We'll give Holly a few more minutes then. I said I'd feed Mr Drouth as well. He's just putting the Grete Herbal back in its case." Liddy tipped the end of a bottle of red wine into the casserole and returned it to the oven.

218

Callum foresaw problems, and hunger. "Can't I just have a bit of bread, to put me on?"

"Help yourself."

Liddy picked up two weighty-looking plastic bags bulging and purple with blackcurrants. "I picked these while I was waiting nervously for you" she grinned at him, "I'll just put them in the downstairs freezer till we can jam them, and by then hopefully Holly'll be in."

She nudged up the latch of the kitchen door with her elbow, and Callum, raiding the bread crock, heard her unbolting the cellar door. A thought struck him.

"Any ice cream left down there?"

He followed her out of the kitchen, chewing. The cellar door stood open. Liddy did not answer so he stepped onto the top of the dimly lit stone staircase and peered down.

Then the light went out.

Somewhere below him Liddy screamed.

"Ma! You alright?"

Callum felt his way down the stairs. His heart bumped in his chest. The air was hissing in his ears. It shouldn't be this cold.

Then he heard it.

A long, withdrawing rattle.

Then a pause.

Then a whoosh, of returning water.

219

He bumped suddenly into Liddy, standing on the bottom cellar step. She gripped his arm. It was pitch dark.

The sounds came again.

Callum's nostrils filled with cool air, and salt.

"It's the sea. In our cellar" said Liddy. "But how -"

"Probably not good" said Callum quietly, "Oh waily, waily -"

An almost full moon appeared from behind what he could now see was thick cloud. What had happened to the cellar ceiling? He looked down at his feet.

The cellar steps ended on a shingle beach which stretched away to either side of them. He watched the tide rush in, almost to the foot of the steps, covering the beach with a thin layer of dark shining water. Then it fell back, rattling on the pebbles. The two bags of blackcurrants lay lapped with sea foam on the beach where Liddy had dropped them. They shone wet and lumpy in the pale moonlight.

"I don't like this" breathed Liddy softly.

Her fingers dug into his arm.

Callum froze, listening intently.

"Shh!" he whispered.

He had not imagined it. He could hear footsteps. They were crunching on shingle. Coming closer.

"Who's that?" hissed Liddy.

Callum stared rapidly around him in the half-dark.

He dragged on Liddy's arm, pulling her off the cellar steps and onto the shingle. He had seen a dark corner, unreached by the moonlight, just alongside the descending cellar steps.

"Shh!" he repeated, as quietly as he could.

His mother obeyed him, which was the most alarming thing of all.

The footsteps were very close now, but their owner was still in the cloud shadow. Callum strained his eyes to see along the beach.

A tall, black figure, striding heavily on the pebbles.

The man approaching them emerged into bright moonlight about a dozen yards away. Numbly, Callum recognised Doctor Sliddery.

His eyes seemed to rest on Callum, and then pass by. Callum remembered that Doctor Sliddery hadn't been able to see him before, in his own time. Perhaps he still couldn't, and couldn't see Liddy either. Or perhaps they were really well enough hidden.

Doctor Sliddery's tall black boots climbed the cellar steps in the moonlight, just level with Callum's face. Their heels clicked and grated on the stone staircase.

Callum turned to Liddy, and put his finger on his lips. He took hold of her hand and tugged.

Now the Doctor was almost at the top of the cellar steps. He had not looked back.

Let him not look back.

Let him not lock the cellar door.

Callum moved out of the shadows and onto the stone steps. Sea water splashed his legs. The tide was coming in. He began to climb, thankful for soft soled trainers.

Once he glanced back to see that Liddy was behind him. Under the moon her face looked very white.

Sliddery pushed on the half-open cellar door.

He did not look back. Silently, with effort, Callum got the very edge of his trainer against the door frame as Sliddery swung the door shut after him.

The door closed, but his foot prevented it from latching. Callum held his breath. As long as Sliddery didn't turn round.

He heard Sliddery's steps crossing the hall.

Warily, he peered out of the cellar door into the 21st century and just glimpsed the edge of Doctor Sliddery's long black coat swinging through the door of the Gardening History Room.

# 33    A Black Plume of
Crows was Rising

"Hawthorne, what - actually – are we going to distract the guard with?" asked Holly, when the branches of the hawthorns had stopped swaying after Callum left.

"Something that such men do value," said Hawthorne, and burrowed once more under the stretched skins of the bender.   She emerged with a small leather bag, its top threaded by a thick leather lace.   Holly, Ana and Sparrow watched silently as Hawthorne pulled open the bag, and tipped out five thick golden coins onto the palm of her hand.

"Sovereigns," Sparrow murmured.

Ana drew in her breath.   "But that is your gold, Hawthorne.  You do not owe the Ursari."

Hawthorne looked at her steadily.   "You forget my daughter."   She looked quickly at Sparrow.   "Your enemy, and mine, are one.  I would not see Lev suffer at Doctor Sliddery's hands."

Holly itched to actually hold a sovereign.   They were fatly shiny, and clinked together musically in Hawthorne's palm.   She watched Hawthorne pour them back into the leather bag and briskly tug the lace to close it.

Hawthorne looked at Sparrow.

"The safest place for you is here, wee one.  Bide here in the clearing while we fetch Lev."

Sparrow's face tightened. "I'll not stay here alone. Doctor Sliddery might find me. And you might nae come back for me."

"I'll always come back for ye" said Hawthorne. Her eyes were troubled.

Sparrow stepped closer, and wrapped her arms tightly around her mother. They all heard her say:

"I'm nae staying here."

Her small face was pinched, eyes squeezed shut as she pressed herself against Hawthorne's skirts.

Hawthorne shook her head slightly, then put her arm around the child. She looked up at Ana, then at Holly.

"I cannae leave her either." She pulled Sparrow upright and looked into her face. "Ye can come. But you'll not go into the Tollbooth, you hear? Ye'll lie quiet in a close near at hand, understand me?"

Holly watched Sparrow nod earnestly.


After a short rest, they were back on the track to Wigtown again. Holly could recognise its landmarks this time, even in the half-dark. She felt very weary, plodding along with one hand loosely around Drum's rein, just below his hairy jaw. She glanced back at Sparrow, who was riding, which seemed fair enough. Sparrow sat loosely in the saddle, apparently lost in thought, winding her Red steadily round and though her hands.

She only looked about nine or ten. Perhaps she was older. It was hard to tell, and the dimness, and Sparrow's white-streaked hair made it harder still.

Holly worried about Callum going back to Liddy without her. It wouldn't take long before Liddy got really concerned about her. Then she would ring Stan. Holly began to chew at the side of a fingernail as she walked, setting her teeth against a little edge of skin.

Ana was walking ahead with Hawthorne, the tassels on her shawl swinging rhythmically with her stride, her back very straight beside Hawthorne's more bulky figure. They came down a little hill into a dip between young birch trees. Ana stopped.

"I fetch the bear." She said it quite calmly, matter-of-fact.

Holly felt chilled. No reason. Except the bear.

She remembered that Drum didn't like the bear either. She quietly took a firmer hold of him as they waited for Ana, who was walking away through the birches towards a small stone byre.

Hawthorne stepped closer to Holly and Drum and put her hand up to Sparrow. "Dinnae mind the bear. Ana knows him. She had him from a cub."

Holly tried a grin, and said, "Well I expect the guard won't like it either."

They waited in silence. Then Drum shifted his legs and Holly felt a tremor run through him. His head went up, and Hawthorne quietly touched Holly's hand on the rein, telling her without words to let go, and Hawthorne put her own hand there instead.

"Stand fast now my galloway," Hawthorne said to Drum. Holly saw Drum's nostrils open, flaring as he breathed more quickly.

Ana was just visible in the dim light, walking back to the track. Her bear lolloped beside her on all fours, a shaggy shadow.

Ana called to Holly, "You walk with me. Hawthorne will hold the pony."

Holly took a deep breath and moved forward to fall into step beside Ana, on the side away from the bear. She noticed gratefully that Ana held a chain attached to a collar around its neck. She looked up at the pale oval of Ana's face. Ana glanced sideways down at her.

"He is good bear," she remarked. "I leave him in that byre, he wait quiet for me. Is lucky the farmer did not get up too early."

"Would the bear have hurt him?" Holly wanted to know.

"Perhaps not."

"Oh. Would he hurt you?"

She laughed at the thought. "Holly, in his bear head, I am his mother. He do what I say!"

"People don't always do what their mothers say," Holly retorted.

Ana inclined her head. "But also I have words for him."

"What words?" Holly was intrigued.

"It is old bear charm. I am Ursari, remember. I learn it from my mother. She learn it from my grandmother."

226

Ana hesitated, then added, "But I tell you too."

Holly was flattered. "Go on then."

Ana smiled. "I say to him, "*She'enedra shena*". You say it Holly."

"*She'enedra shena.*" Holly smiled broadly back. The bear ignored both of them.

"Why doesn't he notice?" Holly wanted to know.

"You must whisper it in his ear! And you must concentrate." Ana's laugh was infectious now, and suddenly it did seem funny, madly ridiculous, that you had to put your face next to the bear's ear to whisper the charm that made it not hurt you. Ana put her arm quickly round Holly's shoulders and gave her a hug as they walked, and the bear continued steadily in its slightly rolling gait on Ana's other side.

"I have also this!" Ana stopped giggling and patted a small pouch which hung from her belt.

"Hush." Hawthorne's voice came softly to them through the beginnings of dawn birdsong. "You two will wake Wigtown for us."

Holly felt exposed as they passed through the West Port, part of this strange group of people and animals walking down the middle of the wide street under shuttered windows, as the first light slowly strengthened. She heard a door bang shut somewhere and a clang of pans from a kitchen. Wigtown was starting to come to life.

"Wait now, a moment!" Hawthorne called softly.

They all paused on the cobbles of the Mercat. Ana bent towards the bear, her hand on the little pouch at her belt. Holly supposed she was using whatever the charm was. The bear halted, and squatted on its haunches. It looked at Holly out of its little eyes. She looked away.

"Just on this side, wee one, you'll wait safe in the yard." Hawthorne spoke to Sparrow, helping her slide down off Drum.

Holly stood by a pend gateway and watched as Hawthorne led Sparrow and Drum through into a wood yard. There was no-one about. Hawthorne led Drum out of sight behind a wood stack, and then returned for Sparrow. Sparrow followed her obediently out of sight.

Holly turned and looked the other way, across the Mercat's wide, dusty street. She saw the first smoke rise from a chimney in the line of houses and shops opposite. Holly saw that Ana's great eyes were directed towards No. 71. She looked wary, almost poised for flight.

Holly too examined the house front carefully, thinking uneasily of Doctor Sliddery. She picked out the familiar window which would become hers at the start of the 21$^{st}$ century.

The tall trees stood darkly in the middle of the square, clustered close. Their branches must cross each other, Holly thought. She imagined the crows, roosting up there, heads tucked under their shiny wings, strong claws gripping the branches.

"Come now." Hawthorne was back again, alone.

Hawthorne, Ana, the bear and Holly walked together down to the Tollbooth. It was a sturdy stone building, thick-walled, with small windows, and lower altogether than the building that had become familiar to Holly in the 21st century. Looking left along the front, Holly could see a low, barred window set deep in the stone. She touched Hawthorne's arm.

"Is that the window of the Martyr's Cell -?"

Hawthorne's eyes gave her the answer, and warned her to say no more. Ana stopped in the road with her bear. Holly and Hawthorne walked up a low step and paused in front of the Tollbooth door. It was looked colossally strong and broad, and was studded with great iron bolts.

Hawthorne knocked on the door. They waited.

Nothing happened.

She bent and picked up a small stone. She held it in her hand and used it to knock again. This time the sound rang in the quietness of the Mercat.

Silence.

Then a dry, flapping, clapping sound rose and beat behind them. Holly's breath caught in her throat and she wheeled round on the step.

A black plume of crows was rising from the tall trees, streaming into the dawn sky. Their scraping cries filled Wigtown.

But behind the door they heard the sound of bolts being worked open. The Tollbooth door swung slowly ajar

229

revealing an unfriendly, heavy man in early middle age. His face was bristly and unwashed.

Holly saw his mouth shut in a tight little trap when he saw Hawthorne Agnew, then drop open again at the sight of Ana, still standing behind with her bear.

"Let us in," Hawthorne said to him. "We have business with the jailer."

The man's eyes hardened again.

"I am the jailer" he said. "What's it to you?"

"I have a fee for you" Hawthorne said calmly. "I will show you when we are inside." She nodded towards Holly.

Holly felt the man scrutinise her. She stared back at him, willing herself not to look away.

But he raised his hand suddenly, his first and smallest fingers curving up like horns in front of his face.

"She's nae entering here!" His voice rose in alarm. "Something's not right about that yin!" He gazed round wildly and his eye fell again on Ana and the bear.

He smiled cruelly.

"Ye can come in," he told Hawthorne, "wi' her," he nodded towards Ana, "as lang as she leaves yon bear out here – she can leave it wi' that craytur' -" He glared again at Holly, and she took an involuntary step back.

The cruel smile crossed his face again.

Hawthorne looked swiftly at Ana. To Holly's horror, Ana nodded and laid the chain down in the dust. She bent and whispered to the bear, which sat impassively on its haunches again.

Then she walked lightly up the steps to Hawthorne's side.

The jailer stepped back and held the door open for them, and as Ana passed close by Holly she pressed something into her hand. Ana did not look at her.

Then Holly saw them both disappear inside the Tollbooth, catching a glimpse of the greenish darkness within, and a chill whiff of damp stone.

Everything was going wrong. She was the one who should be in there, because she was the one to unbolt the cell door.

The great door swung shut in her face and she heard the jailer crash home the bolt.

A rumbling growl came from behind her.

# 34   At The Martyrs' Cell

Holly was afraid to turn round.

If she moved, it might be enough to make the bear attack.

The rumbling growl came again.

She clenched her fists, and remembered there was something in her hand.

She looked down at what Ana had given her, and saw it was the little leather pouch that had hung at Ana's waist. What was it that Ana had said? "I have also this" – and she had laughed like it was no bother dealing with a bear.

Into Holly's mind flashed an image of a baby Ana tumbling and chuckling among bear cubs. Perhaps that was how the Ursari grew up. A Paddington in a red hat was no substitute when you had to turn round and find out if a bear charm worked for you.

Holly took a deep breath, and turned round.

The bear had risen to stand on all fours. It was strangely still, except for the slow growling which moved its jaw and neck when it breathed. It watched her, without blinking.

Very slowly, almost unable to believe what she was doing, Holly took a step towards it. She put out her hand, dangling Ana's pouch from it. Was it imagination, or did the bear focus on it for a moment? Holly felt her blood pounding in her ears and fought to control her panicky breathing. Perhaps bears were like horses, and knew when you were afraid.

The bear stopped growling.

The sudden lack of growling in the Mercat sounded loud for a moment.

Holly took another slow step forward.

In her head she repeated the bear charm Ana had taught her. *"She'enedra shena"*. *"She'enedra shena"*. The bear watched her silently. She was only a couple of steps away now. If it leapt at her now – she forced the thought away.

She held out the leather pouch. The bear put out its muzzle, sniffing. She moved the pouch closer. It swung on the end of its leather cord, and buffeted the bear's muzzle.

Holly's stretched nerves reacted. Her hand jerked, and the bear, with amazing speed, snatched at her wrist. She felt its teeth close like an iron clamp around her arm. She braced herself for the dreadful bite.

But the bear didn't close its jaws.

Its little eyes stared into hers. *"She'enedra shena"* she thought.

She tried to relax, not pull away from the teeth.

"*She'enedra shena*". It came out as a croak, and she said it again, more strongly.

"*She'enedra shena*".

She relaxed, strangely calm.

The bear's eyes flickered. Then she felt it relax too.

The great jaws unclamped her arm. The bear dropped its head and sniffed again at the pouch. She let it.

"*She'enedra shena*" she said again, softly, bending towards its thickly furred ears. Greatly daring, she picked up the end of the bear's chain. She shortened it in her hands so that the bear could just feel the pressure she had on its collar.

Then she took a step forward, and the bear lowered its head and set off beside her. They walked slowly together along the road in front of the Tollbooth.

Swamped with relief, Holly struggled to think what to do. She didn't dare stop walking. At the end of the Tollbooth she turned back up the Mercat the way they had come. She saw Sparrow peering out from the wood yard gateway. Behind her, an agitated snort from Drum.

"I thought you were going in with Hawthorne!" Sparrow's low hiss sounded alarmed.

"So did I," said Holly in a kind of loud whisper, still walking carefully towards the wood yard gateway. "The jailer said Ana had to go instead. I think he did it just to leave me to be eaten by him". She nodded politely at the bear.

"Aye." Sparrow agreed. "I'll have to walk behind you."

She stepped out into the road, and as Holly passed by the gateway she saw, out of the corner of her eye, Sparrow tugging a reluctant Drum out into the Mercat.

"What will we do now?" Sparrow trailed behind Holly and the bear.

Holly tried to walk calmly, and think at the same time.

"How can we help them?" she wondered aloud, twisting her head so Sparrow might hear her. "I think the jailer might just lock them up too."

"The cell has a window. Come on, eejit." Sparrow struggled with Drum, who was following Holly and the bear extremely reluctantly, his ears laid back. At every step Holly could hear him snort nervously behind her. They all turned at the Mercat Cross and began to walk back down the other side, facing the Tollbooth again.

Holly felt as if cold eyes were watching her, walking slowly down the Mercat in front of the dark windows of No. 71, and under the tall trees full of crows.

She glanced up once, into the still-shadowed branches, but the bear growled softly. Holly quickly concentrated on just walking, just being beside him.

They reached the dusty cobbles in front of the Tollbooth. Holly searched with her eyes for the window, and as they walked she found it again. A low, barred window set deep in the stone, almost at ground level. The cell must be under the Tollbooth.

235

As bravely as she could, she held out Ana's pouch to the bear's muzzle, bent down and said softly, *"She'enedra shena"*.

The bear sniffed at the pouch, and paused, and its little eyes looked up into her face. Holly gave the chain a sharp small tug. "Sit" she said, praying it would work.

The bear hesitated. It lifted its lip in a snarl.

Holly did not breathe. She stared into the bear's eyes.

The bear sat.


"I still have the Knife." Sparrow had tethered Drum to the last of the tall trees, and was standing at a careful distance away from the bear.

Holly looked round and saw Sparrow pulling the bundle wrapped in a dirty rag out of her skirt pocket. Carefully she unfolded the faded cloth, and lifted out the knife she had used when they had all escaped from the Darkment.

The dark blade of the knife gleamed smoothly in her hand.

"What will it do?" Holly's voice came out very small. At the sight of the knife all the noise and terror of the Darkment were back inside her head.

Sparrow smiled, and for a moment Holly did not like that smile. Sparrow showed her teeth, but there was no warmth there.

"It cuts," she said simply.

She walked towards the barred cell window, holding the knife out in front of her.

"There's no glass in it!" Holly exclaimed as she came closer.

"The prisoners would starve if there was glass in it," Sparrow sounded puzzled. She glanced round at Holly. "Their families have to feed them."

Sparrow knelt by the window. "Are ye there Lev?"

"Aye. And I'm not alone! Is that you Sparrow?" It was Lev's voice, but although it was now first daylight in the Mercat, all Holly could see down in the cell was the faint pale oval of a face.

"Wait up."

Sparrow took firm hold of the knife in both hands, and laid the blade to the centre bar across the window. She cut twice, at the top and at the bottom.

The Darkment Knife went through the thick metal like butter.

Sparrow moved on to the next bar, and then the next.

Then she carefully re-wrapped the knife and put it away. Holly dragged the cut iron bars away from the cell window.

Hawthorne was first out. Holly could hear Ana and Lev laughing and gasping as they helped to heave her up onto the high window ledge.

"Nay but I scarce fit through!" Hawthorne was out of breath herself as she straightened slowly up. She stretched up stiffly, pressing balled fists into the back of her waist. Then she put her arms round Sparrow.

Holly saw Sparrow close her eyes, just for a moment.

Ana was next, pausing only to lift her skirts out of the way, then climbing neatly. Last of all, Lev scrambled up and out into the Mercat.

"Are you alright Holly?" Ana asked. "Where is -"

She stared around, then saw the bear sitting a dozen yards away. She smiled broadly.

"You did well Holly."

Holly gratefully handed back the pouch. "What does it have in it, Ana?"

Ana was rapidly re-tying it to her belt. She glanced up.

"Oh, how to say – a seed – no - aniseed?"

Holly nodded.

"And bone," Ana added, "ground up bones of a man who was eaten by bears. Long time ago."

"We need to leave," said Lev, who was looking anxiously towards the door of the Tollbooth. Holly saw that his dark face was grazed, and swollen around one eye. She looked away quickly.

"Get us into the tall trees just now," said Hawthorne. "Do you gather up your bear Ana."

Ana picked up the bear's chain, and spoke to it quietly as everyone moved quickly towards the tall trees in the centre of the Mercat. Holly, hurrying, thought briefly how strangely scary the trees had been a few minutes ago, and how now they were a sanctuary, safety from the jailer in the

Tollbooth.  She headed for Drum, tethered in the darkness among the trees.

Then she noticed that the daylight had changed out in the Mercat.

The pale blue sky was gone.  It looked lower.  The colours had turned to a dark slate grey, streaked with dirty yellow.

"Look, it's got nearly as dark out there as it is in here," she remarked to Hawthorne, who was close behind her.

Hawthorne gave Holly one look, and Holly recognised instantly that there was something not right.  Something bumped her hard in the back.  It was Drum, tugging uneasily against his tether.

"Look – still no-one," said Ana, pointing to the great Tollbooth door.  "We should go.  Now."

Hawthorne looked doubtful.  Holly saw her shake her head, but she untied Drum, passing his reins over to Holly.

Then Hawthorne, her hand in Sparrow's, stepped out of the trees in the direction of the Mercat Cross and the West Port. The way that led back to the bender in the wood.

Holly followed Hawthorne, leading Drum.

She felt a cold wind sting her face like winter as she came out from under the tall trees.  She tried to pull her sweatshirt closer round her neck.  It really was going dark.

Drum switched his tail and stopped dead.  She turned round to him and his eyes rolled at her mulishly.

"Oh come *on*, Drum! Callum's right, you are so -"

She ducked instinctively.

Without warning, the air filled with the black wind of hundreds of crows. They poured from the tall trees, and focused their noisy flight around the heads of Holly's little band of people and animals.

Drum plunged in panic in the raucous cawing. The sound did not diminish naturally. It came on like a wave, withdrawing slightly and then rising again.

Wings clapped around the pony's head and Holly cringed by his plunging shoulder, trying to raise her arms to shield herself, trying not to let go of the reins. She glimpsed Ana crouched over her bear in the road. Ana shrieked at the crows, beating them away.

The birds began to rise a little now, their noise lessening slightly.

Holly looked up and realised that their little group had been driven across the street under attack from the crows. They were gathered now in front of the columns of No. 71's graceful portico. Holly looked fearfully up at the black door, and the crow doorknocker.

Hawthorne was comforting Sparrow. Holly saw Ana smile up at Lev in quick relief, as she brushed dirt from her skirts.

And then from inside Doctor Sliddery's house came a long scream.

Holly froze.

She knew at once, without ever having heard such a sound before, that the person screaming was terrified.

Worse, she knew she was hearing Liddy.

# 35    Beware By Me

Holly began to do the things that needed to be done. She moved numbly, automatically, her mind completely occupied by the sound of Liddy's scream. She could still hear it ringing inside her head. She did not dare think what it might mean.

She found she was looping Drum's reins over a handy hook in the wall by the front door, tugging at Hawthorne's arm to draw her attention, and then seizing Doctor Sliddery's great brass door knob with both hands, feeling the metal strike cold to her fingers. She kept her eyes firmly away from the crow doorknocker.

The doorknob turned smoothly and the door swung open. Holly almost fell into the hall in her hurry.

In front of her was a neat pile of brochures lying on a side table. Automatically Holly read the heading on the topmost brochure: "Wigtown Book Festival 18-30 September".

She stared wildly around her.

In front of her a door stood open into the café. She could see mugs, and a cafetiere, still half full.

She glanced to her left and looked up, checking. Gold Roman capitals over the door proclaimed, "The Gardening History Room".

She looked back.

"Hawthorne – this is now. I mean, we're all in my time. It's all changed."

Hawthorne picked up a Book Festival brochure and turned it over.



"No! No – let him go! Please!"

It was Liddy's voice, breaking with fear.

Holly plunged through the door of the Gardening History Room, and immediately pulled up short.

Mr Drouth was standing directly in her way. He was clutching The Grete Herball to his chest, as if it was a precious baby. Holly got round to one side of him, and stared.

Liddy was standing rooted to the spot. She did not seem to have noticed Holly and the others coming in.

She was holding both hands to her face and Holly realised with horror that she looked quite frantic with fear. Then she spoke again, and her voice shook.

"Let him go. I don't know who you are, but, please just let him go. Please -"

Shock filtered through Holly.

She saw that Callum was there on the other side of the room, near the fireplace. His head was bent to one side, because Doctor Sliddery's arm was wrapped tightly around his throat. Doctor Sliddery, tall in his long black coat, his greasy hair tied loosely back, looked contemptuously at Liddy across the room.

"Ma." Callum sounded faint. "Ma. Just stay back."

"Look, he's just a kid."

Liddy made a visible effort and focused all her powers of persuasion on Doctor Sliddery. "Please let him go. We haven't done you any harm. If you just – please – go away, I won't – I won't ring the cops or anything."

Doctor Sliddery had become distracted by the sudden arrival in the room of Hawthorne, Sparrow, Lev and Ana, all crowding in behind Holly. Holly saw him slightly relax his grip on Callum as his mouth opened at the sight of Sparrow.

"It was you," he hissed, "was it not? You made this thing – the Stone Fire - this evil in my hearth."

He dragged Callum roughly to one side. Behind them was the marble fireplace. Holly stared.

There was no fire lit in the hearth. She tried to remember what Sparrow had said, had that been something about a stone fire, after she got them out from the Darkment?

She looked more closely at the fire. Something green glittered through twigs. Great flat stones lay on top.

"What fire?" Liddy's voice cracked with anxiety. "What's going on?"

Holly's heart was bumping in her chest.

Doctor Sliddery tightened his grip on Callum and addressed Liddy.

"I will take this one. He is fair exchange-" he turned his face to glare at Sparrow "- for that other. And he is stronger too."

Holly saw Hawthorne was just in time to snatch hold of Sparrow as she lunged forward at Doctor Sliddery, her face shut with hate.

Hawthorne had a firm grip round Sparrow's narrow shoulders. Holly saw her raise her other hand to cover her mouth as her eyes explored the Stone Fire.

Unexpectedly Mr Drouth took a step towards Doctor Sliddery.

"I believe I may be addressing one Doctor Jared Sliddery" he said pompously. "If so sir, you are likely to be interested in this – ah – volume?"

Holly realised Mr Drouth seemed to have no concerns about why he should be able to have a conversation with an eighteenth century alchemical doctor, nor did he seem in the least bit concerned about Callum.

She watched him hold out The Grete Herball at arm's length towards Doctor Sliddery.

For a moment Holly caught Callum's eye.

Momentarily releasing his grip on Callum's throat, Doctor Sliddery straightened up in surprise. His eyes were on The Grete Herball. His face sharpened with interest, and Callum moved quickly.

He lunged away from Doctor Sliddery, but before he could reach Liddy long white fingers caught him by the hair and held on without effort.

Holly gasped.

She looked across at Liddy, who for the first time seemed to register she was there. And then, with a quick glance back at Hawthorne, Holly stepped close to Liddy and put her arms around her.


Doctor Sliddery kept one hand tight in Callum's hair, bending his head over. Holly could see Callum biting his lip, trying not to cry out.

Doctor Sliddery addressed Mr Drouth.

"How came you by my property? What you hold is the work of many lifetimes. Step closer to me. I will take my book now."

Imperiously, he held out his free hand for the book.


Holly hugged Liddy, smelling her clean, daffodil skin.

She glanced up, and saw Liddy's eyes, never moving from Callum.

Then she felt Liddy take her hand and squeeze it.


Mr Drouth kept his distance from Doctor Sliddery, but he held up the book in both hands.

"A fine piece of work, Doctor Sliddery." He inclined his head. "But there are errors in it."

Doctor Sliddery's expression grew colder. "You have no idea to whom you are speaking. Do not make me show you what I am. Give me the book."

Mr Drouth stayed where he was, and opened the book. "For example," he said pedantically, "in your chapter on the treatment of ailments of the mind, you advise the use of *hiera picra*. I have to inform you that more recent scholarship would dispute this most emphatically. I – ah – rather think you might be interested to discover -"

Doctor Sliddery lunged forward, dragging Callum, who let out a yell of pain.

Everything happened very fast.

Sliddery caught hold of The Grete Herball in his free hand, and twisted it out of Mr Drouth's startled grip.

Liddy let out a cry of horror, her eyes on Callum.

Holly held on to Liddy's hand and tried to comfort her without words or looks because she did not dare take her eyes off Doctor Sliddery. Beside him, Callum stood bent and twisted by the hand still gripping his hair. Holly could see he was crying quietly.

Mr Drouth spluttered in indignation but stepped back.

The alchemist stood with his feet apart, holding The Grete Herball in one hand, and Callum's hair in the other. His face was alight with a kind of passionate triumph as he gazed down at the book.

247

"I hold it sooner even than I wrote it," he said softly. Holly thought he seemed to be speaking to The Grete Herball, not even to himself. "My completed Herball." His lips curved in a smile. "I have tricked Time. However I must needs continue to cheat Death."

He glanced towards the doorway, filled with people.

Sparrow spoke. Her hair had come loose from its usual binding and its white streaks were very visible.

"You cannae pass over your threshold. I bound you to The Crow House with the Stone Fire."

Sliddery stared levelly at her.

"I wish you ill," he said.

The long frock of his coat swirled as he turned to the window, dragging Callum after him. He raised the book and laid its edge gently on the glass.

The window burst outwards with a soft shattering sound.

Mr Drouth let out a whimper of protest. Close to Holly's ear, Liddy let out a sob.

Holly felt something inside her reach a tipping point, and begin to fall.

"No!" she shouted.

She let go of Liddy and threw herself across the room.

She caught tight hold of Doctor Sliddery's arm, the one holding Callum.

"No!" she repeated, staring up into Doctor Sliddery's face. She made eye contact.

"Let him go! You can take me instead!" She could not stop shaking.

Doctor Sliddery's cold blue eyes burned into hers. She read contempt, but also calculation. She stood, still clutching his arm, still trembling.

He said nothing.

Suddenly he released Callum's hair, with a shove which sent him sprawling on the rug.

Holly felt a hand as strong as a vice grasp her wrist.


Doctor Sliddery clasped the book to him, and forced Holly onto the window ledge. She scrambled up, trying to avoid a jagged fragment of glass sticking wickedly up from the base of the frame.

Sliddery's arm forced her through, bumping her head painfully on the bar of the sash.

Her feet scrabbled for the pavement on the other side.

Then Doctor Sliddery was climbing nimbly out over the window ledge, ducking his head.

He balanced himself by leaning his weight on Holly, stepping smoothly down onto the pavement as she collapsed. He yanked her back onto her feet.

They stood side by side on North Main Street.

The crows soared out of the tall trees, whirling like black smoke.

Their voices grated inside Holly's head.

249

# 36    Mind Well The End

Doctor Sliddery yanked Holly's arm to make her follow him, and she staggered.

"Untie that beast."

In front of them was Drum. He was still tethered by his reins to the ring outside No. 71's front door. Doctor Sliddery gave Holly a sharp push, and she almost fell against the pony's neck.

Drum jerked his head up and pulled the reins tight on the ring, and Holly began trying to loosen them. Her fingers were shaking, and her upper arm hurt where he had held it. She fumbled and tugged.

"Drum, good Drum," she managed to say. Her voice was shaking.

With difficulty she edged him nearer the ring. Her hands worked, and she unknotted the reins. Behind her the crows were still cawing and circling the Mercat in 1797, filling her ears with the dry flapping of their wings.

She turned the frightened pony slightly on the pavement, in front of Doctor Sliddery.

A crow was hopping heavily by his feet, its eye like a polished stone.

"Stand the nag down in the road" he said impatiently.

When she had led Drum off the paving onto the cobbles, so the pony stood lower down, he snatched the reins from her, and seizing her again with his free hand, threw her up onto Drum's back. He was unexpectedly, terrifyingly, strong.

Holly clutched the familiar support of Drum's mane, winding it around her fingers for comfort, trying not to cry with shock.


The front door of The Crow House opened suddenly.

"Holly!" It was Callum, and just for a moment, behind him, she glimpsed Liddy.

Then Doctor Sliddery tightened the reins fiercely with his free hand and heaved himself up behind her.

A corner of The Grete Herball stuck painfully into her back.

Doctor Sliddery laughed.

Drum took off with a bound, his hooves ringing on the cobbles.

Holly clung to his mane, forced forwards onto the pony's shoulders by Doctor Sliddery behind. They crossed the Mercat in a few wild strides. For a moment Holly glimpsed the bear, still squatting where Ana had left it in the tall trees.

Her breath tore in her throat.

"Help me," she begged silently, "Hawthorne – Liddy – please help me -"

But then Doctor Sliddery wrenched Drum's head round so fiercely that the pony's nose almost touched her knee, and she had put all her efforts into clinging on.

Drum plunged wildly, but was forced down a narrow, stone flagged pend between two houses on the other side of the Mercat. Under the low roof the noise of hoofbeats and her own sobs battered on Holly like hammers on iron.

For a second between Drum's flickering little ears she could see the narrow slice of daylight at the other side, and then they burst out of the pend and Doctor Sliddery was hauling Drum round to the left. Bruised and lurching, Holly managed to recognise the back alley behind South Main Street. Drum dropped to a jolting trot on the greening cobbles, his head held high and nervous.

Holly became aware of the smell of Doctor Sliddery, sitting close behind her. Distastefully her nose caught his pungent, thin yeastiness. She glanced down at the arm that encircled her on her left, at the strong white hand gripping the reins, the stiff looking black cloth of his sleeve.

"Where are we going?" she dared.

He jabbed her in the back with the book.

"It is not your place even to ask."

He kicked Drum back into a canter, and Holly clung uncomfortably to her hank of mane. She glimpsed the end of the long back alley, and below it, the grey surge of Wigtown Bay. The hills on the far side were lost in dark clouds.

The loudness of Drum's snort seemed to surprise even Doctor Sliddery. The pony braced his forelegs in a series of uneven bounds as he tried to stop.

On all fours in the gateway at the end of the alley was Ana's bear.

Drum attempted to spin round.

Holly seized her chance and twisted to see behind. As Doctor Sliddery furiously hauled Drum straight again, she just caught sight of Lev and Hawthorne, hurrying along the alley behind them.

In front, the bear lurched up onto its hind legs. Holly saw the pink rawness of its mouth open in a snarl, its teeth white. Then she saw Ana behind it, still and stiff and dainty.

"Let Holly go!" Ana's voice shrilled over the bear's growling.

Holly could feel Doctor Sliddery's anger like air pressure building inexorably inside her ears. He kicked savagely at the pony's flanks and forced Drum forward, forcing him to the left of the bear.

The bear dropped again to all fours and began to run at the pony.

Holly heard her own gasp of horror and then swayed, as at the last moment Doctor Sliddery wrenched Drum to the right.

The bear lurched and swiped. Holly's nostrils filled with its hot smell.

253

For a second she caught a glimpse of a great clawed pad, and then, incredibly, they were past and galloping wildly downhill.

Holly lurched and clung, trying to see where they were going.

"Harbour Road?"

But it was not the Harbour Road Holly knew. Drum plunged down a rutted track that led down through rough grazing land to reedy marshes. Already they were out of Wigtown, and ahead Holly could see the estuary churning through the salt marshes like a coarse brown rope, spreading wider and wider with the incoming tide. Shifting mists hung and blew over the bay.

Drum's gallop pitched and slowed.

Holly clutched his mane tighter and felt his hesitation.

Doctor Sliddery jagged at the reins and Holly felt the impact of his kick to Drum's flanks. But Drum was slowing, nodding his head, dropping unevenly back to a walking pace.

Now Holly could clearly feel him limping.

"Damned tinkler nag!"

Doctor Sliddery slid off Drum's back, and dragged Holly down after him.

She looked back at Drum's near hind leg and recoiled in shock.

His dun coat was split by two long parallel gashes. They oozed blood, which was running steadily down over his hock. He raised his hoof and took the weight on his other three legs.  His flanks heaved, hollowing with his efforts to get his breath.

"The bear -" Holly said.  She put her arms around his sweating neck, appalled at what had happened to him. Drum's nostrils flared noisily in and out.

"Leave the nag," said Doctor Sliddery.

Holly kept hold of Drum but looked round at him. Doctor Sliddery too was out of breath.  He clasped The Grete Herball to his chest, and there was still something arrogant about him, standing very upright in his black clothes in front of Wigtown Bay.

She realised she was angry.

"No. I won't."

"Your way is with me now," he said unpleasantly.

She clenched her teeth.  "No chance."

He lunged forward unexpectedly and diffuse white pain shot through Holly's head.   Doctor Sliddery's fist was bunched in her hair.  He wrenched, and she felt her fingers leaving Drum.   Tears poured down her cheeks and she staggered blindly, stumbling on tussocks, following him with her head down and twisted.

"Hell's biscuits!"

The familiar voice cut through Holly's shock and pain. She struggled to see behind her, leaning her head towards

255

Sliddery's hand, trying to get some of the pressure off her scalp.

It really was Callum. He was running down the track towards them.

"Doctor Sliddery! Let her go! You can't get away. There are too many of us."

Holly tried to speak, but couldn't. She could see Liddy, and Hawthorne, and Lev and Ana, all hurrying behind Callum.

Doctor Sliddery dragged her round to face them. The Grete Herball stuck painfully into her side.

"Get back from me," he hissed. "Or it will go the worse with Holly Berry."

The resonance of his voice as he spoke her name burned through Holly like a branding iron. "I will be like Sparrow," she thought despairingly. She thought of Stan, and Liddy and Callum, and tears closed her throat.

"Let her go," said a high, piercing voice from behind them.

Holly felt Doctor Sliddery jerk his head round.

"Let her go," repeated the voice. "I have – this."

Doctor Sliddery swung round, again hauling Holly painfully with him. She struggled not to fall, and to move quickly enough to keep some of the pressure off her hair.

It was Sparrow.

256

She stood scarcely ten feet away. Behind her the sea was surging into the estuary. She was very pale, and in her hand she held up the Darkment Knife.

"My Knife. You took my Knife from my workbench. You dared -" Doctor Sliddery's breath rasped. "I should kill you now."

He wrenched on Holly's head, but she knew he was no longer thinking about her.

"Let Holly go. Let Holly go. Then you can leave. Then you can *die*." Sparrow's voice filled with sneering contempt. The Darkment Knife glinted dully as she held it up.

"If you dinnae let Holly go, I will run. I will run and throw this – thing – into the salt water. It will go out to sea. The sea will eat the blade. And then you will die anyway, in your own time."

"All times are mine." Doctor Sliddery did not take his eyes from Sparrow, and the Darkment Knife. He shifted his feet, and braced them.

Then the hand in her hair forced Holly forward, and down.

She cried out, and landed on her knees, and felt the rush of his long coat go past her face. One of his boots landed squarely on the back of her hand as she sprawled in the reeds, pressing it down into dark water just below the surface. She spluttered up.

She realised she was free just as she saw him closing on Sparrow.

But Sparrow turned and fled, running barefoot, twisting like a rabbit across the flooding salt marsh.

Doctor Sliddery, still clutching The Grete Herball to himself with one arm, ran after her, stumbling slightly across uneven clumps of reed and soft ground.

Holly saw Callum, Liddy, Hawthorne, Ana and Lev fan out, blocking Doctor Sliddery's return to dry land. But he did not look back as he hurried after Sparrow.

He had nearly caught up with her.

And then Holly saw Sparrow pause, just for a moment, and raise her arm, and then the Darkment Knife was cartwheeling through the air, turning over and over, spinning its dulled shine under the dark grey clouds.

It vanished from sight.

There was a soft splash.

Doctor Sliddery stopped running.

Still kneeling in the cold brown water, Holly watched him. He stood quite still. He stared at the place where the Knife had vanished.

Then she saw him tighten his grip on the book and move away. As he passed by Sparrow she ducked and fled away along the edge of the estuary channel.

But Doctor Sliddery did not look at her. He kept walking, his lank hair lifting a little in the morning wind, his long black coat blowing out at the back.

He stumbled once, and then Holly saw him step purposefully into the broadening water of the tide. It was up to his knees.

The water swelled against him as he went deeper. She saw it lapping at his chest, and saw him lift the book higher. He moved steadily forward into the tide.

A restless mist blew across him, and he was gone.

# 37    Something Very Strange

Holly strained her eyes to see.

Nothing.

Nothing but the grey tide, the dead weight of the sky.


"Are you alright Holly?" It was Liddy.

She moved closer and took Holly's hand between her own and rubbed it. "He didn't hurt you, did he?"

Holly shook her head.

Liddy put her arms around her. "I'm so confused. I don't understand anything I see today, but it was brave of that wee girl to draw him off you. I really don't care what happens to him but I hope she's – oh – she's over there, with that other lady."

She pointed.

With difficulty, Holly realised Liddy was talking about Sparrow, who now stood with her face buried in Hawthorne's skirts.

"And Drum," Liddy remembered suddenly, "He went lame." She turned back towards the pony, her face concerned.

Holly looked round for Drum. He had not moved, and he put no weight on his injured hind leg. His head was drooping.

They hurried back across the rough marsh towards him.

"Oh my God, what's that?" Liddy stared in horror at the blood dripping from Drum's wound. "Oh, poor pony, he needs a vet."

She dug in her pocket and flipped open her mobile.

Callum stepped forward, then stopped.

He caught Holly's eye.

Holly struggled to take in Liddy's grasp of what was going on. She looked round cautiously. Ana stood beside Lev, watching the place where Doctor Sliddery had stepped into the water. There was no sign of the bear.

"There's no signal at all," said Liddy, staring at her phone.

Hawthorne walked back towards Drum, one arm wrapped round Sparrow, to hold her on her hip. She studied the pony's wound without saying anything for a moment. Then she spoke to Holly.

"Our galloway needs care. In my wood I have herbs for his wound. Do you walk on his other side. He will be slow."

Holly ducked obediently under Drum's lowered neck, and Hawthorne took him by the bridle. She coaxed him into a reluctant, almost hopping walk. Holly pushed her left hand up under his mane, feeling the warmth there, and the sweat drying on him. She looked round suddenly for Liddy.

"Liddy. This is Hawthorne. She's going to help Drum." She added, pleadingly, "Walk with us."

Liddy closed her phone slowly and pocketed it.

"Come on ma," said Callum, and put his arm through hers. They fell into step beside Holly.

They had walked a few slow paces when Ana broke away from Lev and came running back towards them.

"Jared Sliddery is dead," she called, "I feel it. The Ursari are avenged!"

She kissed first Hawthorne, then Sparrow, then Holly. Callum recoiled. Ana smiled at him, and then at Liddy.

Then she said softly, "I must find him, my animal, before they go in garden today. He hungry."

"You mean, you left that bear in someone's garden -" Callum's voice died away. He shook his head. "I hope they're late sleepers."

Ana smiled dazzlingly at him, turned away with a rustle of skirts and set off back uphill towards Wigtown. Lev waved at them all, and then caught her up.


"A bear!" exclaimed Liddy.

"Did you not see the bear?" said Hawthorne very gently to Liddy, as she persuaded Drum back into his hopping walk.

Liddy looked carefully at her.

"I was following you and Callum. Down the alley. There wasn't a bear when I got there."

"Good," said Callum shortly.

262

There was a short silence except for their walking feet brushing against grasses, and the uneven, muffled thuds of Drum's limping.

"There's something very strange going on," Liddy said.

"Um." Callum hesitated. "Can I explain later?"

"Ok." said Liddy, thoughtfully. "Ok."

Looking over Drum's bobbing neck, Holly tried to read her profile.

Liddy turned and smiled at her.

"Well, it could be so much worse," she said, "He didn't manage to kidnap either of you. And Drum will get better." She laughed rather shakily. "That – person - only got my book. And then walked into the sea with it. It doesn't matter really."

"Don't you mind?" Holly stared at her, amazed.

"Well I should probably report it. Though Mr Drouth was trying to ring the police from the phone in the hall when I last saw him."

"He was what?!" burst out Callum.

"He doesn't seem to have followed us though, does he? And I never saw any police," Liddy wondered.

Holly turned mutely to Hawthorne.

Hawthorne shook her head very gently.


To Holly it seemed a long, slow walk to Hawthorne's wood. No-one talked much. Drum limped, and blew out through distended nostrils each time he had to touch the ground with his injured leg. Holly's own legs felt heavy with tiredness.

They entered the wood at last along the green track. When they reached Hawthorne's bender she unsaddled Drum and put him in the pen before firmly leading them to the hazel hurdles.

"You'd best be on your way," she said to Liddy.

"But what about Drum?"

"For now, he's best off here with me. I'll see to it he's back with you soon as he starts to heal."

Liddy looked Hawthorne straight in the eye for a long moment.

Then she nodded slowly.

"Alright. Thank you."

Holly hugged Hawthorne fiercely, and tried to hug Sparrow. But Sparrow stepped a little to one side, clinging to a handful of Hawthorne's skirt.

Then Callum and Liddy and Holly ducked out between the hazel hurdles.

"What an amazing little herb garden she has in there. It's funny, but..." Liddy's voice tailed off. She lifted up a long rose shoot to squeeze past it.

Then she added, "I'm sure she'll care for Drum. Though I really don't know why I feel so sure."

She straightened up as they emerged onto the stubble field, and pulled her phone out of her pocket again.

"Ah, that's better, there's a good signal here."

She stopped on the wide stubble field and dialled.

264

"Just thought I'd try the house – see if – oh! Is that you, Mr Drouth?"

Pause.

"No, no, don't worry. I've got them both...Nobody hurt, except... What? ...Yes, he must have been some sort of nutter. Probably did the bookshop damage as well."

She listened.

"The phone was down? You couldn't get through? Don't worry about it. Doesn't matter now." She snapped the phone shut.

She stared for a moment across the field where the hills were bulked on the other side of Wigtown Bay. Then she turned to Holly and Callum.

"Come on," she said. "When we get in we've got to break it to Mr Drouth that The Grete Herball went into Wigtown Bay. It's going to hit him hard. He loved that book."

Liddy shut her phone, stuck it back in her pocket, and put one arm round Callum and the other round Holly.

They began to walk.

# 38    What Happened

Holly stretched sleepily and elbowed the kitchen door open, making the wonkily lettered "Private" sign swing on its hook.  Sunshine filtered in through the conservatory roof, though the weather had cooled noticeably since the weekend. Holly sat down at the kitchen table, and poured herself some juice.  She smiled at Liddy, who sat with her hands wrapped around her coffee mug.

"Sleep ok?" said Liddy.

"Mmm."

"Any sign of life from Callum's room?"

"None.  Is Dad up?"

"Up and out.  He said he wanted to explore before the town got moving."

"He has this energetic streak," Holly mused.

"You feeling ok about school next week?" Liddy asked delicately.

Holly considered.

"Well, fairly. Though I haven't really met any girls yet."

Liddy laughed.  "No, well you did seem to just spend most of the summer outdoors.  With Drum.  Things were a bit hairy till you and Callum started to get on though.  And then they were – a bit hairy." She grinned, then stopped.

"Liddy," said Holly carefully.  "Are you – do you mind much, about The Grete Herball?"

Liddy looked down into her mug, her fingers still laced around it.

Then she said, "I do, of course. It was part of the house. And it's – it was – a part of my business. I suppose for most people, only in the sense that it was a curiosity. I suppose I can always buy another curiosity, but not one with such a direct link to No. 71 and Good Garden Books."

"I'm sorry -" Holly began, but Liddy interrupted her.

"No – you mustn't think that that's important. And what could any of us have done about it?" Liddy closed her eyes for a moment, then continued. "What was bad, what was really bad, was when he – that man – snatched Callum. And then you saved Callum, and he took you. That was terrible."

Liddy's voice shook as she spoke. Holly looked closely at her, and saw that her eyes were shining with tears.

"Liddy," she began, desperate to reassure, "you know, he wasn't, well, wasn't -"

"It's ok, Holly." Liddy sniffed, then quickly put a warm hand on one of Holly's, and as quickly took it away again. "I never did ring the police. I thought about it, then I realised I just couldn't. Because I didn't know who all the other people were. I'd never seen them before, and I haven't seen them since. And because of what happened in the cellar."

Liddy sighed, then shot a look at Holly, who was nodding. "You know about that? Callum told you?"

Holly nodded more.

They were both silent for a moment. Then Liddy continued, "So I don't know. I must have had a funny turn, mustn't I? And who was he? It was something to do with the house, with here? Wasn't it? Because, when I thought about it afterwards, I remembered that ages ago, people in Wigtown used to call it 'The Crow House'."

Holly stared at her.

"Actually," said Liddy, "when I bought it, there was an ugly doorknocker on the front door that was a bit like a crow. It was actually quite creepy. I took it down, it didn't look very friendly to customers. I remember wondering about it though..."

"Where – what did you do with it?" Holly asked.

The front door bell of No. 71 pealed loudly.

"Oh, can't remember - " Liddy got up and left the kitchen, and Holly followed.

"Put it away somewhere safe, I expect." Liddy opened the inner door and then bent to unbolt the big white outer one. Holly helped her haul it open, ready to chock it back for customers later on.

Standing on the pavement was Stan, and he was holding Drum.

As he caught sight of Liddy and Holly, Drum whickered flatteringly, and stepped boldly up with his front hooves on the doorstep under the portico.

"Hey, no further!" Stan grappled with the halter rope he was holding and heaved against Drum's weight.

"Drum! Sweet little Drum!" Liddy hugged the pony's neck.

Holly reached out and stroked his face, breathing in his warm, grassy breath.

Then she trailed her hand down his back as she squeezed out down the step and alongside him to look at his near hind leg.

She let out a gasp.

"Liddy. Look!"

She saw Liddy's smile fade and made space for her as she moved quickly along Drum's side and stared at his leg.

"It's completely healed. There's hardly even a scar."

"But he's only been away a week and a bit," Liddy said.

"What are you both on about?" Stan sounded bewildered. "Does this sort of thing happen often in Wigtown Liddy? This funny woman in several skirts just came round a corner of the track down by the harbour. Then she gives me a pony on a string, assures me it's yours, smiles at me and trips off through the brambles."

"That fits." Callum appeared, and leaned sleepily against the open door. He curled the toes of one bare foot over the top step.

Holly exchanged a grin with him.

Lightning Source UK Ltd.
Milton Keynes UK
UKHW010630030920
369276UK00001B/86